THE WITCH'S GET

Diana Janopaul

Photo Credit–Front Cover: Diana Janopaul
Photo Editing–Front Cover: Kenna Dwinell
Photo Credit–Back Cover: Rachel Dodrill

ISBN 978-0-9840207-0-6

Artemis
Moon
Publishing

Dedicated to:

The women, men and children who were cruelly tortured and executed during the burning years. May their souls find peace.

The wise women in my present and my past—Kenna Blake, Samantha, Lena, Nellie and, perhaps the wisest of them all, Kenna Jane.

Acknowledgements

I would like to thank my kind readers who gave me gentle and constructive criticism and the encouragement to keep working: Steven, Dara, Kenny, Gwen, Dawn, Alina and Stacey. I also owe thanks to the authors of several books I used as reference material: Christina Larner, who wrote the seminal *Enemies of God: The Witch-hunt in Scotland* (1981); Anne L. Barstow, author of *Witchcraze: A New History of the European Witch Hunts* (1995); and Tess Darwin, author of the amazing *Scots Herbal* (1999). These authors should not be held accountable for any liberties I might have taken with the subject matter—it is a novel, after all. Their books, however, were my trusty companions and go-to sources throughout the process of writing *The Witch's Get*. I want to thank my husband for his unwavering support during my moments of doubt and for putting aside his love of the non-fiction genre to read a smallish novel about a midwife. Thanks to Mara and Debbie for making the final product beautiful, inside and out. Lastly, I want to thank Alina Vogelhut Gardner for having such wonderful midwifery karma, for sharing her experiences with me, and for her sweet spirit, which will always be open to seeing the dragon's eye.

PROLOGUE

My name is Samantha, after my grandmother. It is not a Scottish name. You'll not be telling me anything I don't know, if you tell me that. My grandmother was English with an English name. So as not to confuse us, I was called Mancy. The meaning of my name is "one who listens." That is true—I have been listening for as long as I can remember. Not just listening with my ears, but with my heart. I listen to the voices of unborn babies in their mothers' wombs and the song of the heather and the moss. I listen with my hands as well, wounds and fevers under my fingers, broken bones in my grip. Listening is simply paying attention and I do that well. The problem with you, who are still living, is that you don't think that we, on this side, are aware of you. We are. We are paying attention to it all.

This story comes from my paying attention to what is being said about us—those of us who lived during the time when it was not safe to be a woman, not safe to tend those wounds and fevers and broken bones. All sorts of names exist for it these days—the witch hunts, the witch craze, the burning years. It is impossible to put one name to something that was so widespread and lasted so many years. It is equally impossible to put a reason to it. Many have tried. The feminists cry, "It was because they were women." The midwives reply, "No, it was because they were healers."

1

The religious folk say, "They were witches, weren't they? They brought it on themselves." It was, according to the sociologists, theologists, anthropologists, and anyone else who cares to have an opinion, because we were poor, had no power, had too much power, or because we ate moldy wheat. Take your choice. The truth is that it was a little of all of that and none of it as well. There is no explaining away madness and cruelty. They existed then and they exist today.

The one thing that the experts seem to agree on is that with all the records and court proceedings, all the graphic details of torture and confessions, what is lacking is the voice of the witch. Of course, you can read countless confessions of copulation with the Devil and midnight frolicking in the moonlight, but those are not the stories I am speaking of. I want to give you the stories of plants and healing, of loneliness and despair. The voice of the witch will be mine for now. I do not pretend that my voice speaks for us all. If you want Isobel's story, you will have to ask her when you see her. For now, it is my story and that will have to do.

I want to start with the word itself—witch. Were we witches? The trouble with words is that they are just that—words. Sitting by themselves on a page, or hanging in the air after an utterance, they are, in and of themselves, meaningless. Were we witches? I don't know what that means, to be a witch. We were women, wives, mothers. Whatever we were, we still are, and we always will be. Healer, wise woman, *curandera*, *sage femme*, witch, sister—it does not matter what name you put to it. We are still here. Our power, our calling has come through the generations from mother to daughter, mentor to student, crone to maiden. I have been watching a lovely lass of ten or eleven learning the ways from her mother. Together, they break up the beeswax and carefully sort the herbs. They infuse the herbs into oils and blend the wax into a salve. She listens carefully, as her mother explains, but she already knows the essence of it. It is in her bones and blood, passed to her from her mother, as her blond hair and gray eyes were.

Yes, we are still here. I am still here. Listening. Paying attention. This is my story.

CHAPTER 1

It begins, and ends, in Scotland. I will always believe that Scotland is the most beautiful place in creation. The Mayan *curanderas* assure me that this is not true, that there is a river in the south of Mexico with water the color of turquoise and waterfalls of shimmering diamonds. They say if you walk through the jungle, to the top of the mountain, you will find the source of the river and the spirits of the *curanderas* will come to you as eagles to give your soul wings. I do not doubt this, but I think it is only because they have not stood in the Scottish hills among the heather, with the wind slapping their cheeks pink, that they don't agree with me.

So let me start with the day I found the bluebottles. I would tell you that this day was the beginning, but that would be a lie. I should warn you now that I was a tremendous liar. Not by nature, but by necessity. If, at the end, I had been accused of lying constantly and without hesitation, I would have had to admit guilt and hurl myself on the fire. Be assured, I have no need to lie anymore—all I tell you is true—but, at the time I was quite adept at it and it served me well. At any rate, I hadn't meant to gather that day. If I had, I would have taken a basket or, at least, worn my plaid or an apron. As it was, I was wearing William's old tunic and breeches. Having slept in them the night before, I had been too lazy to change. I was not expecting to see anyone that day, unless Annie happened to chance by and she had already seen me wearing William's clothes. She didn't remark, just raised that one crooked eyebrow the slightest bit. Of all the accusations flung at me later, they missed the fact that I had taken to wearing men's clothing as much as possible. It was more comfortable, but mostly it kept me from being lonely. It felt as if William were still with me a little when I wore his clothes.

As I said, I didn't intend to gather. It was a glorious day. On these new spring days, I could feel the tightly bound knot that lived in my stomach begin to relax and uncurl—one tentative strand and then another. It wouldn't take much to ball it up again, a sound or fleeting thought would do it, but for a moment I could breathe and feel light, almost happy. I only meant to walk the path up to the crest of the hill and then return to the cottage before dusk. I had promised myself to cook a meal that night, not just an egg broken over some porridge, but a proper meal of cabbage and barley stew. Since William had gone, cooking a meal for myself and then sitting to eat it was a lonely undertaking. Usually, I stood to eat—a scoop of cold porridge, a boiled egg carried to the garden. Tonight I would sit.

Then, there they were—the bluebottles. They were just off the path, as I crested the hill, hundreds of them. I always thought it an omen of sorts, finding a plant in such great numbers or of such brilliant color. Experience had taught me not to ignore them when they presented themselves in such a manner—I had regretted passing them by on more than one occasion. I inched down among the bluebottles, as if they might scatter with a sudden movement. Isobel had taught me to pray as I gathered, "In the name of the Father and the Son, I do this work." Isobel had always liked things done a certain way, that being her way, so with her I did as she instructed. But, when gathering on my own, I didn't utter this prayer. It seemed awkward, stiff—not the kind of talk for friends. Instead, I chatted with the bluebottles, thanked them for their beauty and healing power. I gathered as many as I could hold in the front of my tunic, taking care not to harvest too many from one area. When I could hold no more, I headed down the hill toward home.

My promise of a proper meal was put aside. I decided on the walk that I would dry most of them, so they would be useful later as teas or poultices. Laying them all out on the table, I grouped them in small clumps. I cut twine to tie each of the little bouquets and hung them upside down from the beam that stretched across the cottage. So many bluebottles dangled from above that I had the sensation of standing on my head in a field of blue. Smiling, I took the few fresh flowers remaining, and floated them in a basin of water. By morning, the water would be a delicate shade of violet. I wasn't sure what I'd need it for, but that would no doubt come clear soon.

Darkness had fallen by the time I finished. I stoked the embers of the fire a few times, ate a scoop of porridge, and climbed into bed, wearing the same clothes still. Drifting into sleep, I played with the bluebottles in my mind. I saw them on the hill, a sea of blue undulating in the wind, and right before falling into sleep, remembered they were used to tend fevers and wounds.

CHAPTER 2

I awoke to the squeak of wagon wheels outside the cottage. I lay still, scarcely breathing, waiting. It seemed unlikely that they would come for me in the middle of the night. The men of the Kirk were doing God's work, and therefore, felt perfectly justified in carrying it out during the light of day. Still, what else could it be? I closed my eyes and willed myself invisible. I have since heard of wise men, yogis, who live in caves and can enter such deep meditative states that they slow their heartbeats to almost nothing. I, of course, knew nothing of this at the time, but when needed, I could slow my breathing and begin to feel myself melt into my surroundings.

Footsteps came toward the cottage, heavy booted steps. Then pounding on the door. I remained still, blending into the linen sheets of my bed. More pounding, then a voice.

"I need help. We have a wounded man."

I didn't reply.

"I know you are there. Your neighbor sent me here. She said you could help."

Annie! Still, I said nothing.

"Please, at least look at him. He will not make it much longer."

The problem with being given the gift of healing is that it is

6

difficult to deny. Since I had come to this cottage, this village, I had vowed not to be involved, not to heal. But, inevitably I was drawn in, unable to suppress it. I had hidden my talent for as long as possible, but after I helped Annie's youngest through a bout of croup, there was no keeping it secret. Annie, an open, loquacious woman, could not fathom my need to be invisible and solitary. Soon, knocks came on the door at all hours. A child was ill or a baby on the way. I refused some at first, but always went to the births. I had seen what damage a panicked father or inexperienced pair of hands could do to a baby. My hands, although large like a man's, were designed to cup the crown of the baby's head as it slid into being. I was a good midwife.

Eventually, I could refuse no one, but did refuse payment. My logic was that if I were not paid to heal, then I could not be accused of healing. Instead, when payment was offered, I would mention that I was in need of more wood, or that my oat supply was running low. And when I found myself up to the rafters in oats, but lacking in beeswax for salves, Annie would do bartering for me in the village. I would not have survived but for Annie.

The pounding began again. I went to the door and cracked it open. The man was startled, in mid-pound with his arm in the air. "It is my brother. He was wounded."

"I'm not a healer. You'll have to look elsewhere," I began to close the door. He wedged it open with his elbow and the toe of his boot.

"There is nowhere else to look. He will not survive much longer without care. Your neighbor said you could help him."

"She was wrong. I'm not a healer. I would be of no help to him."

"Aye, but you are a woman. By your very nature, that makes you more qualified to tend him than I."

I could not argue on that point. Women make better healers than men. I'm not saying that no men exist who are great healers. But, when you look closely at these men, you realize that they are great healers because they act more like women than men. They listen, they nurture, they use their hearts.

I opened the door fully and walked toward the wooden cart on the path that ran in front of the cottage. The man in the boots followed me. In the back lay a pile of rags and stench. It was a man, but only barely.

"He's already dead," I said and turned toward the cottage.

"No, he lives. Look."

He reached over to the pile of rags and pulled the tunic up to show me his chest, rising and falling in shallow, rapid movements. Above his breast, on his left shoulder, was a gaping wound.

"What made this?" I asked, touching the area surrounding the hole.

"A sword."

"Have you not tended it at all?"

"I brought him here, didn't I?"

I gave him what I hoped was a glare. I ran my hand down the wounded man's chest. His skin was dry and hot under my fingers.

"When did this happen?"

"Yesterday. No, the day before."

"Have you not tended him at all? Any water or food?"

The man in the boots returned my glare and spoke as if I were a particularly dull-witted child. "We are trying to return home. It is obvious that he will not survive the journey. If he dies, so be it. Do the best you can."

I looked more closely. His legs were lying at an unnatural angle to his torso, giving him a twisted, broken look. "What happened to his legs? Are they wounded as well?"

"He said he could ride after taking the blow, but he fell and landed on a log, the trunk of a tree. His legs have not moved since. A few days rest should do the trick."

My mouth must have actually dropped open. I had seen dogs lose the use of their hind legs, through accident or old age. The only thing a few days rest would do would be to render them even more flaccid and useless. One had to kill the animal straight away. It was the only merciful thing to do.

8

"Surely, you can't—"

"Will you tend him or not?"

I hesitated. At least now I knew what the bluebottles were for.

"Bring him inside."

The man in the boots motioned to another who had been standing with the horses at the front of the cart. Together, they lifted the bundle and headed toward the house. I walked ahead and held the door wide.

"Put him there," I said with a nod toward the only bed, as I lit a candle on the table.

"I am prepared to pay for your services."

"I am not a healer. I don't need pay."

"I can see you're not a healer," he said, his gaze resting on the bluebottles dangling from the beam. "Nevertheless, I am prepared to pay you."

"I do not want your money."

His jaw muscle twitched. "It is *not* for your services. It is for his keep. If he dies, you will have to bury him and if he lives, you will have to feed him."

In the candlelight, I could finally examine this man in the boots. He was tall with dark hair and brilliant eyes. It was hard to discern by the soft light, but I imagined they were a clear green. He was handsome, but his features were hard. I could detect no kindness or humor in him at all.

I matched his tone in my reply. "If he dies, I will bury him myself and if he lives, we'll make do with what we have."

"As you *wish*." He spat the words at me, as he turned on his heel and, without even a glance toward his brother, strode out the door, his companion close behind.

The door slammed behind them and I held my breath as I waited for the stomping of their boots to the path. They paused outside the door and, for a moment, I thought that perhaps he had changed his mind and would come back in to collect his brother. In the short time from the pounding on my door until now, I had already developed a sense of protectiveness about this wounded man, probably as reaction to the lack of consideration he received from everyone else. I had still not exhaled, when finally they returned to the cart and left. I unballed my clenched fists and allowed myself to breathe again.

I didn't understand then, of course, how having this man deposited in a heap on my bed would change everything. If I had, would I have tried so hard to save him? Of course, I would have. How could I have not?

CHAPTER 3

Isobel always said that if you don't know where to begin, sit for a moment and think. That just goes to show the difference between us, me and Isobel. She would sit and think, but I sit and don't think. I sit and feel. I am able to feel wounds and illnesses. They talk to me and tell me what they need, just as my plants talk to me and tell me what they do. So, I pulled the low stool over to the side of the bed and sat quietly. Although his legs gave him the appearance of one beyond hope, he was still there, his energy strong. Water would be first and then cleaning.

I poured some water into a small bowl, soaked a scrap of nettle cloth in it, and slowly dripped the liquid into his mouth, between his cracked lips. This was a tedious process. He was not making an effort to swallow at all, and I didn't want to drown the man in my desire to save him. So, we went very slowly, drip, drip, drip. When almost half of the water was gone, I used the damp cloth to wipe the blood and grime from his face and mouth. What color were his eyes? The same brilliant green his brother had? I had the impulse to open one eyelid to see. But, it felt wrong to touch him just to satisfy my curiosity. Indeed, I had the strong impression that every touch, every movement should be with intention to heal. By doing what I could for him, I would have the opportunity to see his eyes later, open and alive.

I brought the candle to the stool in order to inspect him more closely. His hair was long and matted with blood and filth. I instinctively wanted to clean it, rinse it with nettle tea and brush it out, but it could wait. His face was relatively uninjured, with just a bruise over one eye. I worked his arms out of his tunic and pulled it over his head. The wound was angry and oozing. Some of the fabric of his tunic had stuck to the edges of the wound and was ripped off when I removed his shirt, causing bleeding anew. The rest of him—arms, chest, belly—other than being caked in dirt and blood, was unscathed.

The stench of his leggings let me know that his bowels had functioned at least once since his fall. There was also the unmistakable acrid smell of stale urine, which was a good sign, considering how little water he had been given. The leggings were not redeemable, so I felt little guilt in using my shears to cut them off him. But, first I had to remove his heavy leather boots, like his brother wore. It was no easy task, one I finally accomplished by bracing myself on the plank that was the foot of the bed and pulling with all my strength. They didn't give easily, but finally slid off. They were as filthy as the rest of his clothing, but of too fine a quality to discard. I placed them near the door for later cleaning. As for the leggings, I held them at arm's length, looked around the cottage, and, finally, threw them outside until the morning. I would bury them then.

He was naked, his top half covered in blood and dirt and his bottom half covered in feces and urine. It was then I noticed the flute. It must have been tucked into his leggings and fallen onto the bed when I cut them off. It was a beautiful instrument, perfectly turned with a delicate inlay of wood of different colors. I had seen many flutes in my life, but none as exquisite as this. It felt good in my hands, smooth and cool. I thought of bringing it to my lips, to try to coax out a few notes, but couldn't bring myself to do it. Instead, I tucked it under the mattress, in the same place Maggie used to keep her coins.

I brought the basin of water with the bluebottles soaking in it. It was cold, but would be his bath. I cleaned him with the nettle cloth, wiping away the excrement and urine last. After throwing the cloth outside with the breeches for later burial, I tucked a dry cloth between his legs and used one of William's tunics to cover his chest. William was stockier than this man, but shorter in stature. The tunic sleeves landed above his wrists by several inches, but at least it would keep him covered. I rummaged in the trunk for one of the sheepskins I had used for Maggie, to keep her paper-thin skin from bruising and splitting before she died. There were four altogether, and I would wash one every day, after her bowels and bladder had emptied.

I pulled all four out of the trunk. By crooking my arm under his knees, I was able to lift his hips slightly off the bed and slid one under him. I was tall for a woman, broad and strong. I had hated this when I was young, but once I began healing in earnest, I knew that I was strong for a reason. I had called on my strength more than once—to hold a woman in a squat to push her baby out or to help move a grown man, if needed. We are who we are for a purpose. You only have to pay attention to find out what that is.

With the sheepskin under his hips, I ran my hands over both legs. They looked for all the world like normal legs. No injury on them at all. I then thought to look at his back. A deep purple bruise spread across his lower back, evidently caused by the fall on the log.

It was well into the wee hours of the morning at this point, and I needed to sleep. But, how to place him—on his back or side? I wanted to turn him on his side, to take the pressure off the bruise on his back, but decided against it. Instead, I left him on his back, and pulled the blanket over him. He looked awkwardly situated and uncomfortable, although he wasn't aware of comfort at that moment.

Nonetheless, I went back into the trunk for a spare blanket, folded it several times, and placed it under his knees, bending his legs slightly. I covered him again, and started to curl up next to the bed on the floor on two of the sheepskins pushed together. But, I had the same feeling as when Lizzie was dying, that I needed to have her close to me, to feel her hot breath and sweaty body against my own, to hear every inhalation and moan. In the end, I could do nothing for her, but I needed to be there. So, instead of lying on the floor, I put one sheepskin on the stool and one on the bed, next to his chest. I sat on the stool and lay my head on the bed, listening for his breathing and soft murmurs, and fell asleep.

The sounds of the morning awoke me only a few hours later. My back and neck were stiff—I was not young anymore. It used to be I could sit with a woman making her journey into motherhood for hours and not tire, nodding off between pains, sitting bolt straight. But, now, a marked lack of stamina for the long births in the wee hours settled over me, not to mention sore muscles the next day. You all now would not think of me as old—I was nearing forty—but, in my day, it was old. A woman married in her early twenties and became a mother straight away. By the end of her third decade on earth, her life was already laid out before her if she were lucky. If not, life would bestow upon her twists of fate, surprises that usually did not bode well for her future, such as finding herself a widow at a young age with many mouths to feed. It was balancing on a precarious perch, being a woman in those days.

The morning light filtered into the dark cottage. I opened the door for sunshine and fresh air as the putrid odor still lingered from the night before. With the soft light, I studied my patient more carefully. His hair was as dark as his brother's, but a smattering of gray said he was the elder of the two. He was also as handsome as his brother, but with a softer mouth. I pulled down the neck of his tunic to examine the wound. In the light, it looked worse than I had hoped. I chided myself for not tending it better the night before, but it was to be a long day and those few hours of sleep would benefit both of us in the end. Looking back now on the day that was to come, I can see so clearly how it all fit together. How my very being, my strength and ability to heal, William's leaving, my coming to this village and finding Annie and Maggie, ending up alone in this cottage—all of this led to that day. That day was created so I could be there to save him. And I saved him, so that he could save me, for in the end he saved my very soul.

I needed a plan. I would make a poultice from the bluebottles. I would also use them in an infusion with comfrey, to be given as a tea. Burning the wound crossed my mind, but no. The wound had been opened for several days caked with filth. I didn't want to close it before making sure it was properly cleaned. For this same reason, I chose not to use comfrey as a poultice. Comfrey heals wounds so efficiently, miraculously knitting the skin anew, that on a very deep wound, it can heal the surface before the inside, causing a pocket that can fill with blood or pus. I would use comfrey in a few days time, after the wound had healed from the inside out. Heart o' the earth also called to me, perhaps mixed with goldenrod in a salve, but I didn't have those in my wooden chest that held the little linen bags of dried herbs. I would have to leave the cottage to gather them, and I didn't think it wise to leave him just yet. With any luck, the bluebottles and comfrey would do the trick.

I put water to heat on the hearth and untied several of the bluebottle bundles from the beam. I crushed the azure petals into a paste, adding a wee drop of warm water. This I placed directly on his wound, covering it with a damp piece of linen. With the rest of the water, I began the infusion of bluebottles and comfrey. Usually, I would let it steep for several hours, but he needed it sooner. I would use this batch after an hour and set another to steep for later. Waiting for the tea to steep, I turned my attention to his back and legs. I did have chickweed in my chest, and that was what the bruise on his back needed. Fresh would have been better, but I was doing the best I could, just as his brother had commanded. I soaked the dried chickweed in some warm water and then poured it onto a wet cloth. Trying to disturb him as little as possible, I slipped the compress under his lower back, directly on the bruise. I then spent some time with his legs. There was no poultice, salve, or infusion that would restore movement to those quiet legs. They were not in need of chickweed, comfrey, or bluebottles, or even my precious nettles, which cured so many ills. I had helped Isobel remove a leg once, rotting and putrid. It was a horrifying task, but only one of many horrors I would eventually face. These legs, however, were not gangrenous, just still. I had cared for one other man who had broken his back in a fall, and he had not lived more than a few days. This man seemed strong, despite his wounds, but it would take more than that for survival. It would take constant care and more than a little bit of the providence Annie always went on about.

After the poultices were in place, it was time to give him the infusion, which was a problem, as he was unconscious. I remembered when Lizzie was very young, vomiting over and over and I sat with her head in my lap and spooned liquid into her mouth, a wee bit at a time. I poured some of the infusion into a bowl and placed it on the stool next to the bed. Then I climbed into the bed, cradling his head in my lap, taking care not to disturb either the poultices or his position. Scooting down further toward him, I lifted his head, so that he would not end up breathing in the infusion, instead of drinking it. Spoonful by spoonful, I poured the infusion into his mouth. Thankfully, he was unaware of the process, as I have had more than one complaint about the taste of my infusions. The most pleasant-tasting herb can't help but become bitter when steeped for so long. Even a generous dose of honey did little to improve the taste—one simply had to bear it.

We spent most of the day like that, his head in my lap, taking a spoonful at a time. I got up to change the poultices a couple of times, then climbed back into the bed with him. I found myself stroking his hair, the way I used to stroke Lizzie's. It was still filthy and matted. I would cut it the next day, if he lived, and then use a nettle rinse to bring out a shine.

If he lived.

CHAPTER 4

He did live. He lived through that first day and then the night. I slept on the floor next to the bed, waking from time to time to listen to his breathing. He lived through the next day, too. The wound, amazingly enough, did not fester, but began to heal. I continued using the bluebottle poultice, and added a bandage of moss wrapped in linen to help absorb the weeping of the wound. He did not wake, but continued to swallow sips of tea and uttered the occasional word. I was not worried that he still slept. The body heals best when we sleep, when our minds are not busy with the worries of life, of being awake. But for his legs, I did worry. It was not natural for legs to lie in one position—they are meant to move about. The logical part of me wanted to turn him, to shift his position, but the other side of me felt he needed to be completely still, at least for a few days. I would have to move him eventually—bedsores and a host of other ailments come from lack of movement. As a kind of compromise, I massaged his legs softly and shifted them slightly, sometimes propped at the knees, other times stretched out flat.

Caring for him required so many decisions that I was unprepared to make, each one carrying with it the weight of his survival. More than once in a moment of uncertainty and fear, I considered giving up, letting him go. If only Isobel were here to give me advice, to talk things through. Instead I talked aloud to myself, arguing with no one about whether to move him and which herbs to use.

Through this all, I neglected the rest of my life, such as it was. I left him only to collect the few eggs my hens produced and spend a few minutes keeping the garden from total ruin. Annie dropped by once, while I was yanking weeds from the kale patch.

"You're needed in the village. An accident at the smithy."

I looked up, impatient to finish and return inside. "I can't go, not today. I'm much too busy."

Annie glanced around my yard as if the source of my newfound occupation might present itself suddenly. "With what?"

"I'm putting up herbs. I've delayed much too long and will lose them all soon."

Annie eyed me, sideways on, raising that one crooked eyebrow. "All right. See you later then?"

"Aye," I said, distracted, already back to my work. I returned to the cottage as quickly as possible, not allowing myself to breathe until I saw his own breathing, deep and regular under the blanket.

My intention of cutting his hair did not come to pass until several days later. I was, at first, overwhelmed with the amount of care he required, like a new mother feels after the birth of her first bairn. A long time had passed since I had cared for a new one and I had forgotten the exhaustion that sets in toward the end of the day. But, as a woman eventually shifts into the rhythm of motherhood, I settled into our routine by the end of the third day. And just as a new mother follows the cues her baby gives her, winding the schedule of her life around her wee one's needs, I learned to follow his body's cues, massaging him and giving him infusions when he was restless. When he fell into a deep sleep, I slept as well, stretched out on a pallet next to the bed, as I did with Maggie.

But, by the fourth day, I could bear the tangled mess no longer. I used my shears on his hair, once quickly to rid him of the worst gnarls and then slowly to make him presentable. I cut it like I cut William's, using my fingers as a guide, only much shorter for easier keep. Afterward, I wiped it through with a rag soaked in nettle tea. I took the rest of the tea outside, leaned forward with my long brown hair dangling almost to the ground, and poured it over.

As much as I hate to play favorites with my plants, I have to admit that nettle is my most cherished. Isobel always called her by the Scottish name, heg-beg, but she is also known as stinging nettle or devil leaf. How the name of the Devil ever became associated with this most healing of herbs, I will never understand. She will sting you, to be sure, but she will also strengthen your blood, give you soup and tea, provide you with sheets and cloth and even feed your animals. I always leave an infusion of nettles with a new mother, to build her blood and milk. She is not the most beautiful of plants, but definitely the most nurturing. The Native American healers here call her "sister spinster." Maybe that is why I love her so much—we have an affinity for each other, sisters in solitude.

The early days of caring for him now seem like being in a dream. I practiced my craft on him with wild abandon. He was a compliant patient, no fussing about remedies or refusing to follow my instructions. It had always confounded me that a person would call for my help when ailing, but would not do what I said to get better. I have noticed that this has not changed over the centuries, people are still as hard-headed as ever.

As I had dedicated every fiber of my being toward his survival, I am still not sure why it came as such a surprise when he awoke. I had left the front door open for fresh air and was beginning to put up the dried bundles of bluebottles, at least all that were left over. I didn't even notice that Annie had stepped into the cottage, holding several eggs in her hands.

"I brought you some eggs. We had extra."

I reached for the eggs, but she still clutched them in her hands, staring over my right shoulder. I had almost forgotten about the presence of a strange man lying in my bed—he had become such a part of my daily existence. I turned to see if the house was on fire when, following her gaze, realized that she was staring at him.

"There's a man in your bed."

"Aye," I replied, in a whisper. "It's William. He's come back, but he was wounded. He's been resting several days."

It always startled me how quickly I could concoct a lie. And how easily it fell out of my mouth.

"Your husband?"

I nodded.

"When did he come?"

"Five days ago."

Annie's blue eyes grew wide with comprehension. "He was the man in the wagon? I had no idea when I sent them to you. What lucky fate is that?"

I could feel my lie beginning to unravel, too soon. "What did they tell you that night?"

"Who?"

"The man with the dark hair. The man in the boots."

"Nothing, just that there was a wounded man. I sent them to you straight away. I knew you would help. There's providence for you. William is home."

"Aye, providence." I didn't much believe in providence, but was willing to credit it, if it would speed Annie's departure. "The eggs, Annie," I said, reaching out again.

"Oh, here they are. Should I stop in again tomorrow? I'll want to know how he is doing."

"Not tomorrow. I'm trying to keep him quiet."

"Well then, the next day?"

"Perhaps," I said. "Thank you for the eggs."

Annie finally took her leave. I happened to glance at the bed as I set the eggs down. His eyes were open, wide and staring. I screamed and missed the table entirely, yellow yolk and white shell covering the stool and floor.

I stared at him, my hand covering my mouth. "I didn't know you were awake."

He turned his head and looked at me with the brilliant green eyes I had been so curious about. He said nothing for such a while that I wondered if the fall had damaged his mind as well as his legs.

Finally, he spoke. "We're married?"

He had heard the lie I had laid out to Annie.

"Well, in a manner of speaking. You're William, my husband. For now."

"And can you tell me the name of my wife?"

He smiled weakly, but I couldn't tell if his words were spoken in jest or ire. I learned later to watch the lines around the corners of his eyes to tell when he was joking. They crinkled with humor. His eyes always gave him away.

"I am Mancy."

"Mancy. That is not a name."

"It is. It is my name. Well, Samantha actually, after my grandmother."

"Ah, after your grandmother. Well then, Mancy, can you tell me how I came to be here, married to a woman with an English name?"

"Your brother brought you, five nights past. You were wounded. I have been tending you."

"My brother. Did he say when he would return for me?"

His brother had not mentioned returning at all and I had not thought to ask. "Actually, no. I'm not sure he expected you to live long enough to return for."

He smiled weakly again. "No, he would not have been so optimistic. You must have tended me well, for here I am."

"Here you are."

He closed his eyes. Our brief conversation had tired him.

"You should rest now," I said softly.

"Absolutely. You told Annie I needed rest."

"Aye, I did and you do. No more talking."

He was silent for several moments, fallen into sleep, I thought. Then, almost as an afterthought, he said, "So, I am William."

21

"Aye, you are William."

"It's a good name."

It was. A good name for a good man.

CHAPTER 5

I was only sixteen when I met William. Isobel and I had been called to tend to a child, one of William's younger siblings. By that time, I had been learning with Isobel for almost five years. When I first started, she only allowed me to help her gather and dry the herbs. I was also expected to cook for her and help with her chores, which I did gladly. It was unpaid labor, of course, but I never thought to object. I was happier away from my home and my father anyway, and happiest when working with my beloved plants. As I grew older, she allowed me to infuse the herbs into oils, and eventually, I learned to make salves. We often used butter for the salves, but they were greasy and turned rancid very quickly. The best salves were made from beeswax. Then it went on smoothly, with no grease, and lasted for at least a year without spoiling. Beeswax was not always easy to come by, though. Isobel didn't let me touch the beeswax for many years. The commodity was too precious to be ruined by my inexperience.

Finally, when I was sixteen, she let me accompany her to a healing. I was to do nothing, say nothing—just watch, and hand her whatever she asked from her box of herbs. When we were called to William's home, it was only the third time I had been allowed to go with her. As I had practiced being invisible from childhood, I was quite good at blending into the background, not being noticed. It caught me off guard, then, that William kept sneaking glances at me. Were my clothes not properly fastened? Had I grown horns on top of my head? It was inconceivable that anyone would pay attention to me, least of all a handsome young man. Later, on the way home, I asked Isobel if I had done something wrong to have attracted his attention.

She laughed and said, "Child, don't you know when a man likes what he sees, he's going to have to look."

Flabbergasted, I argued that she was wrong, that there was nothing for him to like about me.

"We'll see," was all she said.

We returned to William's home twice more. The child had suffered a broken collarbone and Isobel wanted to make sure it was knitting well. Each time, William was there, silently stealing glimpses in my direction. It occurred to me later that it was unusual that he should be there, at home, in the middle of the day, when all of the other men were in the fields working. At first, I thought that it was the admirable concern of an older brother, but now I know he was there for me.

If William had been someone else, someone less patient or more forceful, he would have never won me. It took him some time after those few days in his home before he actually spoke to me. I was on the path, heading into the hills to do some gathering, when he stepped in front of me. He had been waiting.

"I'm William," he said. "You were in my home. You helped with my brother."

"I remember," I replied. I had no experience talking to men. I rarely spoke to my father, as few words as possible when it was necessary. My brothers, although growing, could not yet be counted as men. The only other men I was in company of were either patients of Isobel or the fathers of patients. Those men rarely even looked at me and never addressed me directly. Poor William had his work cut out for him—I didn't respond to him with more than two words put together for the longest time. But, he was patient.

He took to meeting me on the path and walking along beside

me on my way to gather. He talked about this and that, his family, the harvest, not waiting for my response, not expecting one. He always left with the same words, "See you tomorrow, Mancy." I would nod and continue on my way, dazed by the steady stream of conversation and still unsure as to why he wanted to walk with me, day after day.

This went on for months. A less patient man would have given up, or a more forceful man would have wanted too much from me too soon. I found myself relaxing into these moments, looking forward to his meeting me on the path, eager to hear the news he brought of the village or his home.

One day, as he was taking his leave, instead of saying, "See you tomorrow, Mancy," he said, "I want to marry you, Mancy." Marry me? I stumbled, almost dropping my basket. He had never made any romantic overtures, had not ever intimated that he was in love with me, had never even taken my hand in his. But, that was William for you, simple and open, straightforward as a man could be. I said "yes" before I realized that my mouth was opening to respond.

I never regretted it. After I met the other William, I realized that there was something lacking in our marriage, an intensity of passion that would later so take me over. But, he gave me so much I had never had in my life. He loved me unswervingly, listened to me attentively. He never lifted his voice or a finger toward me. He was solid, a safe haven during those tumultuous years of grief and pain. It is no wonder that when he left me, I panicked, grasping for handholds on a cliff with a face as smooth as glass.

CHAPTER 6

With my lie to Annie, this man, this new William and I began our time together, the pretense of being husband and wife added to our relationship of healer to patient. I watched him as he slept, the bluebottles forgotten. He had not tried to move, to sit up during his brief wakefulness and he had surely not yet comprehended what damage had been inflicted on him by the fall. I dreaded the moment when that horrible realization would come over him. As difficult as it was to be a woman in those days, being a man was not much easier. There was no understanding, no compassion for those weak or debilitated. A man without legs was useless in every way.

He slept until dusk. I left him only once to wring the neck of one of the few chickens Maggie had left me. I counted on them as my source for eggs and was not inclined to eat them because of that. But, now awake, William would need something more substantial than tea. I would start him with a broth and, if that caused him no ill, would give him some of the flesh as well. I was stewing the meat off the bone when he awoke for the second time.

"Something smells good."

"Broth. Are you hungry?"

"Aye, I am. Will you help me sit up then?"

I stirred slowly, not looking directly at him. "Did you know you had a fall off your horse?"

"No, I don't remember that, only taking the blow."

"Your brother said you fell onto a log. The trunk of a tree, he said. You landed on your back."

William knitted his brow, his head tilted. "So it has been my back you've been tending?"

"Your back, your shoulder, your legs."

"My legs were wounded also?"

I shook my head, placed the spoon on the table and pulled the stool next to the bed. I sat on the stool and looked into his eyes. "Your back was injured by the fall. That, in turn, has injured your legs. They don't work properly."

"What do you *mean*?" He began to push himself up on his elbow. "Help me sit up."

I pulled back the sheet, exposing the still naked lower half of his body. Then I climbed behind him on the bed, hooked him under his arms, and sat him up as much as possible. He was not really sitting, as he was leaning back considerably against me. Still, it was the most upright he had been since he came to me. He had not said a word since I moved the sheet. He reached down with one hand and touched his right thigh. He jerked his hand back and held it in the air, as if he had touched something filthy and didn't want to contaminate anything else with it.

I did not see the expression on his face, but in my mind I have imagined it over and over again. He said nothing, his hand still suspended in the air.

Finally, I reached for his hand and placed it directly over his heart. "Still beating. You're still alive."

"It would be better if I were not."

I didn't argue.

"Will you let me send word to your family? That you are here and alive? I'm sure Annie knows someone who could go."

"No. No message. I'll not go home like this. I'll not be pushed home in a cart. If I go home, it'll be on my own legs."

"But that might be a very long time." Or, never. "They could help you better than I, send for a surgeon. Or… something." I was struggling for the right words. "I did promise your brother to take care of you, and I will do my best. But, I wish you would let me—"

"On my own two legs. Not before."

I reached under the mattress for his flute. He didn't take it in his hands, so I simply laid it next to him on the bed.

CHAPTER 7

I had seen the face of despair many times before. As a healer, I was present for the most intense emotions in life—the joy of birth, the unrealistic hope of a mother for her sick child, the agony of a man on the death of his wife. Despair presented in different ways. Some people railed against it, others wept through it. William simply let it take him over.

He stopped speaking, wouldn't respond to my queries. He would let me give him tea and broth, but very little. He allowed me to tend him, clean him, turn him, but it was like tending an empty husk.

This silent grief was not something I could slap a poultice on to fix. Although I had suffered much grief in my own life, it had never been given full rein. We were not allowed to mourn my mother's death, not allowed to mention her name again. My father, not a kind man before she died, became unbearable afterward, cruel and drunk. We all learned quickly not to talk about her, even my two year-old brother knew not to ask for her. I survived by understanding what my place was, what was expected of me, what boundaries were set for me. I was to do my chores, look after my brothers, and stay out of my father's way. As my brothers grew, they were able to keep themselves out of trouble, and I had more time to be alone, to sit in the hills.

This is when I learned to love my plants. I would sit and listen for hours, sometimes talking to them about my mother, the little I remembered about her. I would try to conjure her face in my mind, but over time it became less defined. She was the opposite of me in appearance. Much shorter than I have grown to be, she would have only reached my shoulder at my full height. She had small hands and a tiny waist. The only thing we would have shared as women was an ample bosom, which was much more proportional on me than on such a wee woman as she was. The rest of her was lost in my mind—her smile, her eyes. I did remember her voice, soft and lilting. She sang constantly, a habit I inherited. Only, I didn't know any of the words of her songs, just the melodies. After she died, there was no one to teach me the words.

I accepted my later losses—the children, William's leaving—much the same way I accepted my mother's death, resigned, no arguing. There was no time for despair, it was not allowed. So, this pervasive, desperate grief of William's scared me in a way I wasn't prepared for. I had never seen someone just give up like that.

This must have gone on for several weeks. The more he refused to live, the more I insisted that he must. He was regaining his strength physically, but was emotionally out of my reach. I didn't know if any hope existed for his legs, but I did know that he couldn't possibly recover unless he wanted to.

It was high time for a change. I got him to sit up on the side of the bed, with his legs dangling over. I pulled the table over close, so he could take his tea and soups properly. In addition to turning him, I began to move his legs for him, in the manner of walking, while he was lying on his back. All of this he bore without complaint, but also without any spark of desire, any enthusiasm.

Every night, after dinner, I would work with his legs, applying compresses and rubbing them with oil. I had no idea of healing them—it just seemed they needed to be touched. I would heat the oil on the hearth, next to the fire. I tested it on the inside of my wrist and when it was warm, would massage the entire length of both legs and his feet. One night, I managed to overheat the oil. I had become distracted with crushing some of my bundled herbs while I waited for it to warm. I poured some into a shallow bowl to let it cool so I could handle it without scalding myself.

Humming a wordless tune, I began to rub the oil into his right thigh.

He flinched. "Careful, woman. It's too hot."

I stared at him. "What did you just say?"

"I said to be careful. It's too hot. You'll burn me."

"You felt it. Your leg twitched."

He said nothing.

I continued massaging. "Can you do it again? Move your leg?"

"No."

"You haven't even tried. How do you know? You'll never get better if you don't try. Try."

"Damn you, I am trying. I've been trying since you poured boiling oil on me."

It was the first time, the only time, he raised his voice to me. I said nothing, but took the bowl of oil to the table. I couldn't decide if I was more hurt than angry and finally settled on a little of both. I moved the bowl back to the hearth, muttering all the while.

William was definitely more angry than hurt. "If you have something to say, say it so I can hear."

"I said that the oil wasn't boiling, just barely warm, but if you want boiling, I'll be glad to oblige. A few more minutes ought to do it. Then we'll see how fast you move those legs." I was quickly heading from hurt to furious. I picked up a spoon from the table and pointed it at him, punctuating the air as I spoke. On the final syllable, the spoon flew from my greasy hand and sailed in an arc across the room. I suddenly felt very silly, standing there with my hand in the air, as the spoon clattered against the wall. I smiled in spite of myself.

William smiled as well. "First, boiling oil. Now, she's hurling spoons at me. Honestly, I thought you were supposed to be caring for me, not killing me."

"It wasn't boiling. And I am sorry I missed with the spoon."

"I'm sure you'll have another chance."

I pulled the bedding over his legs and began to prepare him for sleep. "You can joke, if you like. But, this is good, William. A good sign. You felt it. You moved. You're getting better."

William shook his head. "It was one twitch. I can't make it happen again. I'll not hold out a false hope."

"All right. But, promise me one thing."

"What?"

"Keep trying. Don't give up. Promise?"

"Aye, I promise. If you promise no more boiling oil."

I laughed. "No more boiling oil. I promise."

I said no more about his legs. I continued our routine, trying to engage him in talk, but after the incident with the oil, he had reverted to his silence, responding when necessary, but no more. I didn't want to push him even further away, so I bit my tongue every time my mouth opened, about to beg, plead, or cajole him to move. Instead, I spied on him, out of the corner of my eye, as I went about my day, hoping to catch a twitch. I thought I was being stealthy.

"You're not fooling anyone, sneaking around watching me."

"I'm not sneaking. I'm just paying attention to how you are doing. It's what I do. Besides, if you would talk to me, let me help you, I wouldn't have to sneak."

"So you were sneaking."

I sighed. "Call it sneaking, if you will. It makes no matter to me. Whatever you call it, if you'll just talk to me, I won't have to do it."

William pulled back the bedding so I could see his legs. "All right. This is it." He scrunched up his forehead in concentration, but then he glanced at me. "It's not much."

"It's all right."

"I don't want you to be disappointed."

"William. Show me."

He drew a breath, scrunched his forehead again, and bent his right leg at the knee, placing the bottom of his foot flat on the bed. He moved it back again and shrugged. "I told you it wasn't much."

"Not much? It's so much more than I thought. I was afraid… I mean, I thought… I thought…"

William finished my sentence for me. "You thought that I would never move my legs again."

"Aye, that was my fear."

"Well, it's a long cry from walking. And I can only move the right. No matter how I try, the left won't behave."

"But, it's a start, William. And far better than nothing."

"No, it's just a wee bit better than nothing. No more than that."

No sense in arguing. I snuffed the candle and lay on my pallet for sleep.

CHAPTER 8

In the middle of the night, came a knock on the door. It was a father searching for help from the midwife. I told him to wait for me outside and closed the door to dress and gather my things. There was no wearing William's clothes for this, so I put on my dress with apron and plaid, and covered my head. I opened the wooden chest to contemplate which herbs needed to go with me. Nettles, of course, and, after a few moments of consideration, mother's heart also. I tucked my things into my plaid, and turned to William. His back was to me, but I knew he had been awakened by the commotion—I could tell by his breathing.

"I have to go out. It shouldn't be long. It's her fifth."

He didn't respond.

"You should be all right while I am gone. I'll turn you now—don't try to move yourself." I leaned over and rolled him onto his back.

"I don't expect I'll be moving anytime soon. One leg won't get me far," he replied and I thought how foolish I had been in speaking those words.

"I'll be back soon."

The father was waiting for me by the front door, sitting on the woodpile. He led the way down the path. Thankfully, he was a taciturn sort, for I didn't feel like chatting. I had always

34

loved walking in the moonlight to a birth, the sounds of darkness enveloping me; the cacophony of bush crickets, the rustle of the trees, the nighttime songs of the plants.

The birth went smoothly and quickly. I began my infusions immediately upon arrival, one of nettles and one of mother's heart. The mother was in the most intense part of her labor. She needed very little from me, so I sat quietly on a stool by the bed and waited. As each pain came, she began a moan deep in her belly that would crescendo and peak with the rhythm of the contraction. As the pain would subside, she would slip off into herself until the next one. Looking at her, I marveled at how relaxed some women are during this process, letting it take them over, instead of fighting against it. Of course, not all reacted that way. I had seen one woman run from her cottage, as if trying to flee the impending birth. She had had four children in six years and was not anxious for another. I chased her out the door and managed to catch up with her at the garden. She squatted and there among the cabbage and kale, I reached down and caught this sweet bairn, saddened that his entrance into this world was not a welcome one. I was worried that the mother would reject him, but once I handed her the baby, she stood and with cord still attached, walked calmly back into the cottage. I cut the cord and she put the little one to breast, along with the next oldest on the other side.

The moans intensified, coming more quickly and lasting longer. I closed my eyes and listened—the moans were beautiful, sensual. I smiled. If someone happened by at that very moment and heard her sounds, they would think that they had caught her in the middle of making love, at the very height of her pleasure. Birth is a sensual process—people always think of the pain, and there is pain, indeed. But, with the pain there can also be pleasure. The first time I attended a woman whose moans were so sensual, I had the feeling I was trespassing on a moment as intimate as that of conception must have been. I caught the baby, cleaned up after myself and went home to wake my husband to make love. "It was a good birth," was all I said. After that, if I woke him upon coming home, he would smile wryly and say, "Good birth?"

A new sound brought me out of my thoughts—the sound of a catch in the throat at the height of the moan. With the next pain, the catch turned into a grunt. She would push soon. I laid out moss covered with clean linen to catch the fluid that would come with the birth. The baby slipped out easily into my hands not long after that. The afterbirth came and then the bleeding began. Bleeding was not unusual for a woman who had given birth many times before and, therefore, was not totally unexpected. But, it is still a shock to see so much blood cascading from a woman, seemingly unending, no matter how many times you have seen it before. I used my hands to squeeze her womb tight, to help staunch the flow, while her husband spooned the mother's heart infusion into her mouth. What a beautiful name for that herb! It is also called shepherd's purse or lady's purse, but at a birth I always called it mother's heart, for that is what it healed. The bleeding eventually slowed, and then stopped. I cleaned the mother and baby, changed the bedding and cooked some broth for the mother. It was well into the morning before I began my way home.

I always slipped into a timeless place during my healing work. Hours flew by or moments dragged out for eternity. My walks home were spent bringing myself back into the world, back into reality. I had not given any consideration to William or his well-being while at the birth, but upon nearing the cottage, I began to wonder how he had fared for such a long time alone. Surely, he was fine, I told myself. I walked in the door to find him lying on the floor, face down and shivering with cold.

"What have you done?" I asked, helping him move onto his back. "I told you not to move."

"I reached for the jar. I leaned too far."

"You shouldn't have reached in the first place! I *told* you not to move."

"I didn't want to wet my clothes."

I had worried that he would have no control over his bodily

functions, but within days, he could not only sense the need to urinate, but could also control it. I found an old jar that I had stored salves in until I had broken the lid and kept it close as a kind of chamber pot. Not close enough, evidently, for him to reach without my assistance.

"I would much rather deal with a wet bed than a broken bone. A wet bed is easy to change."

I pulled the stool over and placed it flush up against the bed. I had not had to lift him since he came to me and I wasn't sure how to proceed. The stool was more than half the height from the floor to the bed, and luckily, the bed itself was low to the ground. The hardest part would be lifting him from the floor to the stool. I sat him upright and leaned over him from the front, but quickly realized that lifting him from behind, under his arms, would be the easiest.

"Let's get you back into bed and in some dry clothes." My anger dissipated, gone as quickly as it had come. I moved the stool out from the bed. Standing behind William, I leaned over, grabbed under his arms and tried to lift him onto the stool. I managed to lift him off the floor somewhat, but not anywhere high enough to get him on the stool. I hiked my skirts higher around my thighs and tried again, this time using the strength of my legs. He was a large man, muscular and broad, and I simply was not strong enough to lift him.

I sat on the stool for a moment to think. I could go for Annie, but hated to involve her anymore than necessary. I could put him on the pallet for the night, but that would just prolong the problem. Eventually, I would have to figure out how to move him on and off the bed. All I needed was a little extra leverage.

"William, can you give me some help? With your right leg?"

"I don't know, Mancy."

"Well, it's worth a try. Otherwise, you'll be sleeping on the floor tonight." I was trying to get a smile from him. "The cold, hard floor."

He didn't smile. But, he nodded. "I'll try."

I pulled my skirts up over my knees again, dropped into a

deep squat and grasped him firmly under his arms. I had held many a woman in this position as she pushed her baby into the world, but never a grown man with useless legs.

"All right. Here we are. Now, plant your foot."

He bent his right knee, as he had done in the bed, and placed the sole of his foot on the floor.

"When I say, push." I took a breath and steadied myself. "Now, push!"

I don't know how much force he was able to exert, but, this time, I lifted him well off the floor. Unfortunately, the stool skittered out from under him and I ended up dropping him with a thud, right on his tailbone.

He winced. "It's no use, Mancy. It's not working."

"Aye, it'll work. One more time. Last time."

I got into position again, but this time I anchored the stool with my foot, and in one movement, lifted him straight up as I pulled the stool under him. I climbed backward onto the bed.

"Hold the stool with your hands." I dragged him and the stool back against the edge of the bed. Lifting him from the stool to the bed was much more easily accomplished with William pushing with his right foot again. We ended up lying on the bed, him directly on top of me, cutting off my breath.

"Oof, you're heavy. And wet. And did I say heavy." I laughed as I rolled him off me.

"Beg pardon," William muttered into the bedclothes, as he was now face down.

I helped him turn over and pulled him up to the head of the bed, poured some water into a basin and put it on the stool. I began to unfasten the drawstring of his soaking breeches. Like my husband's tunic, the trousers were ill-fitting, too wide and too short, but they were what we had. I loosened the string. But he grabbed my hands and held them tight. "Please don't."

"Please don't what? I have to change you. You can't lie here cold and wet."

"I'll do it then." He maintained his grip on my hands, while I still held the drawstring tight.

"You can't. You won't be able to get them past your hips. I have to help you."

He looked at me, his lips set tight, and shook his head.

"Don't you think I haven't seen everything you've got already? I have rubbed, wiped or cleaned every spot of skin you own. I vow I know your body better than my husband's." I spoke lightly, with humor, all the while untying the drawstring and lowering his breeches. "And I have to say it isn't much different than all of the other bodies I have rubbed, wiped, and cleaned. And there have been many."

He stopped resisting my efforts, but placed both of his hands over his face while I cleaned him. I didn't understand his shame, when I had spent so much time caring for his body before. But, later, when I thought about it, it was obvious. He was no longer the empty husk I had cleaned and turned, but a man who was trying to fend for himself and he had failed.

I cleaned him and changed him into dry pants and then wiped up the floor. I had turned him on his side, toward the table. I put some porridge on to cook—I was slowly feeding him heavier foods. I was tired from the birth and needed to sleep a little, but he needed to eat first. I sat at the table and put my head into my hands to rest.

"So, you really did have a husband?" he asked quietly.

"Yes, of course. Is that hard to imagine?"

"No, not at all. I just wondered, well, I thought—"

"You thought I was lying about that, too."

"It was a thought. Where is he?"

"He left, went to look for work. I was going to be with him, but I only made it this far." I got up, stirred the porridge, and pulled the stool next to the bed. I hesitated. "I don't know why I told Annie you were my husband." I shook my head. "No, that's not true, I do know why. I can't just have a man lying here in my bed, whether I am tending him or not. I needed you to be William."

He ran a finger across his eyebrow. "Do we have any children?"

"No, no children." I said.

"Do we love each other?"

"Yes. Yes, we do. We did."

He nodded and then fell quiet. I stood and spooned some porridge into a bowl for each of us and put it on the table to cool. "He played the flute, too. Like you. His was not such a fine one as yours, of course. It was very plain, but still beautiful."

"Do you have it? I would like to see it."

"No, he took it with him. To keep him from being lonely, he said."

I leaned over the bed to lift him to a sitting position and then swung his legs over the side. As I was straightening myself up, he grabbed my hands in his. "You should have let me die. It would have been better than this."

I answered slowly, carefully, "I thought about it. It wouldn't have taken much. You were not good."

"Why didn't you?"

I tucked a stray lock of hair behind my ears. The truth was it came to me several times during that first day of caring for him that it would better if he weren't to survive, that survival for him would be more of a punishment than a gift. But, each time the thought crossed my mind, I would remind myself that I had yet to see the color of his eyes. The thought of those clear green eyes kept him alive.

"I don't know. It is not in my nature, I suppose."

I leaned over and kissed him on the top of his head. "Time to eat."

CHAPTER 9

William did not ask me much, at first, about my life. I did not want to know about his. I did not want to know if he was married or had children, where he came from, or even what his true name was. I preferred living with the pretense we had strung together. My life was so full of lies at that point that the truth seemed like an unnecessary burden, one I was not prepared to bear. We settled into a routine that revolved mainly around his care, turning him, moving his legs, cleaning the sheepskins and bedding. I also had to continue caring for the garden and chickens, although I admit that I did as little as possible to get by. I had no time for the solitary adventures I loved so before. Walking in the hills and gathering my herbs were not part of my schedule. They occupied too much time and took me away for too long from the cottage. I soon found myself becoming worn, stretched thin, from tending to everything but myself. I had been used to being alone for some time and had quite enjoyed the freedom of not having to cook, clean, or even change my clothing if I did not have the inclination to do so.

To be sure, William was not demanding. He rarely asked for anything. It was purely my own doing that I imposed on myself an expectation of caring for him, nurturing him as I did. Maybe it was an outpouring of the love I would have bestowed on my husband and children, if given the chance. Becoming a mother was not easy for me, for my body. How ironic that women would come to me for help when they couldn't conceive, yet I couldn't seem to carry a pregnancy. The first two times I did not lose the pregnancy, the little ones were born too early and both only lived a day, a year apart. Our first born would have been named Thomas. It was my fourth pregnancy. I carried Thomas longer than any of the others, but not long enough. He was born in the bitter cold of December, several weeks too soon. He stayed with us a few hours, his translucent skin deceptively pink. I thought I was impervious to loss, but I knew nothing of the despair of losing one so well formed, so beautiful. I was devastated. Five months later, I was thrilled and horrified to realize I was carrying another. This one would have been called James. He came into the world during the same bitter cold as Thomas, one year and two days later. He entered with his hand leading the way, above his head, as if testing the waters of life. Isobel swears that he never was truly with us, that he never drew breath, but I saw him look at me, just for a moment, and for an even briefer moment, he looked around the cottage. Then, as if to say, very politely, "If it is all the same to you, I'd rather not," he closed his eyes and joined his brother. I never told anyone, not even William, about his decision to leave us. He would have worried that I would feel rejected. But, it wasn't a rejection really, just a demure declination of what had been offered him.

Years later, after more heartaches with each loss, I gave birth to Elizabeth. Isobel tended me during my confinement and welcomed Lizzie into her hands. I never knew that I could love any one being so much as that wee one. William and I both adored her, spoiled her no doubt, but how could we not? We had waited so long and had suffered so much. I was finally a part of the universal gathering of women who are mothers. Finally, I was able to nuzzle her head and inhale her delicious aroma. To feel my breasts fill when I heard her stir, and then sit for hours, suckling her by the hearth, kissing her feet, as she would drift to sleep, drunk from my milk. I loved being a mother, being her mother, more than I could have ever imagined. It was all taken from me too soon. I was inundating this William, my new William, with what was left.

Self-imposed as it might have been, the strain of caring for him day in and day out was taking a toll. William noticed it before I did. I had fed us both for the evening, changed the sheepskin and cleaned him, cleaned the pots from cooking, and was turning him one last time. I usually awoke several times during the night to turn him, left side to back and then back to right side. I probably could have let him go through the night, but always judged what I needed to do for him by what I would have wanted done for me. Surely, I turned more than three times in the night, as most people do, and I couldn't bear the thought of him having to suffer in one position, uncomfortable. As it was, I was turning him onto his left side, facing the table, to begin the night.

"You seem tired," he said. "You should rest more."

I looked at him in disbelief. "How can I rest more? I can't rest at all." I was exhausted and on the verge of tears. Surely, he could see how difficult it was to care for him. I cared for Maggie during her last few months, but up until the very end, she could get up and move about. Even when I had to lift her, it was a sight easier than lifting this grown man.

"Why don't you sleep in the bed, next to me? After all, we are married. Nothing wrong with sleeping next to your husband."

The thought of not having to sleep on the hard floor was tempting.

"It would be easier to turn me during the night. And you know I won't bother you." He looked away. I tucked my hair behind my ears and without saying a word, climbed into the bed, my back to him, and fell asleep immediately.

I had a dream that night. I was walking on the path, overcome with fatigue. My feet were weighted, each step a phenomenal effort. I wanted nothing more than to lie down right there on the path and sleep. But every time I lay down, I would be walking again, plodding along toward something. On either side of the path, were all of my friends—chickweed, bluebottles, nettles, and others I did not recognize. As I walked past them, they swayed and bowed to me, as if to say, "We are not what you need. Keep walking." I continued, now on a path that I don't know during the day, but one that I often visit in dreams. It always took me up the same green hill, along the crest, and then into the woods. This time when I exited the woods, I found myself in the most beautiful field, covered with dandelions. There were thousands of them and all were dancing in unison, vibrating, almost humming. I began humming with them, dancing with my hair long and loose, laughing and singing. It felt so good. I was alive again.

The next morning, I left early to gather dandelions. Isobel called them piss-a-bed and she used them when someone was having trouble, not peeing enough or peeing too much. She taught me to eat their greens, cooked in a stew and to steep the flowers into a tea. Like my precious nettles, dandelions nourished those of us damaged, not only physical hurts, but also wounds of the soul. I found them, in abundance, not far from the cottage and was able to return to William quickly.

The wonderful thing about dandelions is that you can use all of the plant—the roots, leaves, and flowers. I sat William on the stool at the table and together we began sorting the leaves from the flowers and rinsing the roots. I wanted to make some infusions of the root right away and brew some tea from the fresh flowers, and bundle both to dry for later. I hummed as we worked, remembering the humming of the flowers in my dream. Whether it was a good night's sleep on the bed instead of the hard floor, or the promise of the dandelion's healing tea, I already felt rejuvenated.

There was a lightness about William, also. He talked easily, asking questions about what we were doing. I had not worked side by side with anyone since Isobel died. Isobel loved to chat while we were working, about this or that. I didn't mind it at the time. After all, it was all I knew. Later, after she was gone, I worked alone for the first time. In the beginning, I missed the company, but soon grew to appreciate the quiet. It allowed me to truly put my intention into my herbs, to gift each remedy with my intent to heal. I did this with words, at first. Over my salve of heart o' the earth and goldenrod, I would speak something like, "May you heal wounds," and over my infusion of mother's heart I would speak, "May you quell the bleeding." As the months passed, I spoke less and less, letting my intentions flow from my heart, silently. I would work in silence for hours, sometimes days.

So, it was odd to be working with another person again. William spoke now and then, but unlike Isobel, he didn't chat idly. He only spoke about the matter at hand. I liked that.

"Gently," I chided him, as he handled the delicate flowers. "We don't want to hurt them."

"They're weeds, Mancy. They don't have feelings."

"Oh, and how do you know? Every living thing has feelings. And they're not weeds. They're friends."

"Well, it must have hurt their feelings deeply to have you yank them up by their roots."

"I asked permission, first. And I only take a few from one area. And I do it *gently*." I slowed his hands down again, as he sorted the leaves from the flowers and roots.

He shook his head, as in disbelief, but I noticed that he slowed his movement anyway. He made me laugh once, out loud, when he placed a dandelion chain he had woven without my noticing around his neck. It was child's play, at the hands of a grown man.

As I laughed, the door opened and in came Annie. She never knocked. William looked at her over his shoulder, dandelion chain still around his neck. I stifled my laugh.

"I just wanted to see how he was," Annie explained. "Better, I see."

"Much, thank you," William answered.

Silence. I was thinking of inviting her in for some dandelion tea when she said, "I won't be staying then. Come down the path to visit sometime."

It always baffled me why Annie took up so much time with

me. I didn't encourage her friendship in any way. It wasn't because she was lacking as a person, I just did not have the place for a friend in my life. She never seemed to notice my indifference, though. The less I did to encourage her, the more she came around. She brought messages to me from families who wanted my services. She bartered for me in the village. She shared her food with me and I think she might have given me one of her bairns, had I expressed an interest. She had more than enough of those—there were always a few hanging off her hem and at least one, sometimes two, on the breast. It never occurred to me, as a person who attempted to be alone as much as possible, that she was lonely. I understood loneliness—on many a night I had to fight away that hollow feeling that hung just over my shoulder, behind my back. The difference between us, me and Annie, was that my loneliness was self-imposed, chosen purposefully to evade other, more unbearable fates. Her loneliness was a creature of its own doing. It invaded her life. Uninvited, it snuck in through a crack in the wall or under the door and took root among the children and animals, staring at her and mocking her. She tried to deny it, perhaps. After all, how can a person be lonely when sharing a small cottage with four or five children—I never could keep count—and a husband. Nevertheless, there it was, always lurking about.

So, she came to me with offers of friendship and food. I was too wrapped up in my efforts to survive to notice how much she needed me. Even at the end, her thoughts were to save me, to help me. I was blind.

She turned to take her leave, but spun around once again. "I heard you laugh, Mancy. When I came in. That was the first time I have ever heard you laugh."

"I'm sure I have laughed before."

"No, never," she said. "Not for me." And she glanced once more at William before she left.

William and I finished our work in silence. I cooked dandelion greens that night for dinner and we drank our tea. I didn't mention to him that, in addition to strengthening body and soul, piss-a-bed was famous for cleaning out bowels. We healers, and we all here agree on this, are unique in that perfectly normal functions of the human body that seem to repel most folk are strangely attractive to us. We gaze intently at pus-filled abscesses, sniff the dried stumps of umbilical cords and monitor what goes in and what comes out of the body without a second thought. For some reasons, humans have a certain reluctance, once beyond the toddling years, to share these aspects of their lives. I have been called to tend men who have refused to let me look at the ailment, especially when it fell under the breeches. Women giving birth seem to be an exception to this. The modest woman will begin her labor fully clothed and covered, only to shed her modesty and clothes as her time comes closer. Women giving birth enter a place where the mind is no longer in control. The body takes over and usually doesn't want to be encumbered with the contrivance of clothing. After the birth, however, she will be appalled that she moaned with the deep-throated sound of an animal or moved her bowels as she pushed her baby out. When her mind is back in control, all of this seems distasteful, unnatural. But, for a healer, the smell of defecation is as natural as the smell of a rose.

William was in no position to maintain any secrecy of his bodily functions. Although we had worked out well how to handle his need to void, the bowels were a different issue. Even though he could detect the need to go, there was no way to do it gracefully. I couldn't hold him up long enough to let him go into a container of any sort.

So, I kept a cloth tucked between him and the sheepskin to catch as much as possible. These were easily washed or discarded. The problem lately was that he was not defecating at all. It didn't surprise me, as he had been given only tea and broth for many days. But, now he was taking solid food. Hopefully, the piss-a-bed would solve the problem, for I really didn't know anything else to do. My worry was that he would, consciously or not, try not to go to avoid the discomfort and embarrassment of having to be cared for like a child. With any other patient, I would have simply told him, "You have to go." But, he wasn't just a patient anymore. Had it happened when I made him my husband or when I started sleeping next to him? Maybe when I pulled him, soaking wet, off the floor. It didn't matter. What mattered was not allowing my feelings to spin any further out of my control.

CHAPTER 10

William slowly began uncovering pieces of my life, delving gently into my past. He was most inquisitive at bedtime, after I had snuffed the candle and climbed into bed. I would almost be dreaming as my head found the pillow, but he would invariably want to talk. At first, I was irritated with him. Then I realized that as full as my day had been with chores and caring for him, his was vacant, waiting for this time, our time together. In the dark, talking was easier, safer. He asked me questions. Why do you wear William's clothes? How old were you when your mother died? Did you know you hum all the time? I found it disconcerting at first. No one, except William, the first William, had ever wanted to know about me, about my life. I would answer him as honestly as possible, which you must realize by now means not honestly at all. Oh, parts were truthful, just never the entire truth at once. Eventually, William, this William, would be the only person I would reveal everything to. But not yet.

The problem was that he attended to everything I said and was quick to pick up on any weaknesses in my stories. The fiction of my life, so far, only had to hold up on the surface. No one, with perhaps the exception of Annie, who I finally figured out saw through all of my lies from the beginning, cared enough about me to match the ends of the threads. The people I had loved and who had loved me—my mother, my babies, William—were gone. I wove them into the deceitful fabric of my past at will, changing their histories to serve me, as needed. I knew they had loved me enough to forgive me. At least, it was my hope that they would.

The other problem was that William was sly. He would wait until I was occupied with rubbing salve on his legs and then would ask a seemingly innocent question. What was William like? When did I come to this village? I would find myself divulging much too much during these unguarded moments. Why was I so distrustful? He wasn't trying to trick me. He had no ulterior motives for asking these questions. He was simply interested in me. I just couldn't understand why.

The salve I used on his legs was of comfrey, that great healer of wounds, used to treat the most recent attack on his body—bedsores. I noticed them one morning while changing his breeches. I had experience with bedsores from tending Maggie and knew how dangerous they were. It wouldn't take much to have one fester out of control. It was a bedsore that ultimately led Maggie to her grave. But, unlike Maggie, William was young and strong and I was determined to keep him alive. I would have to turn him more often and place him in positions that would take the weight off the worst areas, his hips and backside. His left hip was suffering the worst. I most often placed him on his left side, facing the table and hearth, so that we could talk as I worked. He needed to spend more time on his stomach, which left him facing the wall against the head of the bed. We needed a change of scenery altogether.

Early the next morning, I threw open the door and announced we were going outside.

"Outside," William said.

"Yes, outside. You must remember outside. Fresh air, sunshine."

"Well, you must remember that I just can't jump up and walk out there. How were you planning on getting me there?"

"You are going to scoot."

"Scoot."

"Why do you keep repeating what I say? Yes, scoot."

"I'm not sure I know how to scoot."

"You will learn. But, first we must get you down." I stood with my hands on my hips, contemplating my next move.

"Do you want me to tumble off head first?" He was trying to sound irritated with me, but his eyes were crinkling. "That seemed to work last time."

"Let's try something a little tamer. We'll just put you down the way we got you up." I had become quite adept at moving him from the bed to the stool, and moving from the stool to the floor was simple.

He looked up at me from the floor, hunched over slightly, and my heart lurched. He seemed small, almost pitiful. There had been a man, a beggar, in my village who had no legs. He was pushed in a wooden, one-wheeled cart by another man, a relative, perhaps, or a friend. I hated to look at him, not because of his legs, which were amputated at the knee, but because of the humiliation he must have suffered to have to be pushed everywhere he went. For a brief moment, I saw William in that cart, and it broke my heart.

I shoved the thought out of my mind and said, almost too cheerfully, "All right, outside with you."

"Scoot. Sounds easy." He put his palms flat on the floor and lifted the weight of his body, just a few inches. The first time, he just dangled there.

"Move your hands back further. Like this. And push with your right foot." I got on the floor with him and we practiced together. After a couple of attempts, we discovered that it was easiest to move backward, in order to keep the legs out of the way. Lifting and swinging his body back, he moved slowly across the floor. He hesitated at the open door.

"What's wrong?" I asked.

"What if someone sees me, sees us? Maybe this is not a good idea."

"We're just man and wife going out for a scoot. No law against that, is there?"

He smiled. "No, I guess not."

At the threshold, I made the mistake of lifting his legs for him, to get over the wooden plank lying there, and threw him off his balance. He toppled backward, flat, his head barely missing the woodpile. He lay there, winded, but laughing.

"Giving up already?" I teased.

"No, none of it." He turned his head to the left. "I was simply admiring your neatly stacked wood."

"Of course."

He stared intently at the woodpile. "Help me turn on my side."

I flipped him and he reached into the pile, between two logs. "What is that?" He strained toward something.

"It's probably a spider. You'll end up with a festering arm to go with your bedsores."

"It's definitely not a spider," he said, pulling a small leather pouch from the pile.

I sat down beside him, tucking my hair behind my ears.

He handed me the pouch, brown leather with a drawstring, and said, "It feels like coins."

Of course. The slam of the door, the heavy boots pausing by the woodpile. His brother had paid me after all. He must have put it on top of the pile. I had not even noticed. I handed it to William. "It's yours."

"It's not mine. I have never set eyes on it before."

"Your brother. He tried to pay me, but I told him I wasn't a healer and could accept no pay. He said it was for your keep, either to bury you or feed you."

William laughed. "What did you say to that?"

"I told him if you died, I would bury you myself, and that if you lived, we would get by. And we have, haven't we?"

"Aye, we have."

I weighed the bag. From the feel of it, there was quite a bit of money inside. I opened for a peek. It was more money than I had ever seen at one time. Maggie had stored away quite a bit, some of which I was still using, but this was much more than that. "He must have cared about you very much."

William smiled, but his eyes were not crinkling. "I think it is a better measure of his guilt than his care. You'll notice that he has not come back for me."

I nodded. I had begun to hope that he never would. "Well, it's more yours than mine," I said, handing the pouch back over to him.

"It's ours." He placed the pouch in my palm. "Put it somewhere, hide it somewhere. We might need it someday."

I walked into the cottage and, looking around, finally decided to hide it in behind the loose stone at the back of the hearth. I returned outside. "We're not finished scooting. Up the hill you go."

It took more than a few minutes to get up the slight rise leading to the garden. William tired easily—his arms had not been used much more than his legs in the past few weeks. I had placed a blanket by the garden, in the sunshine. We finally arrived at this destination, and I turned William on his stomach. I pulled his tunic up to expose his back to the sun, and after much protesting, he let me lower his pants as well.

"What if Annie comes by?"

"If she had a close look at those bedsores, she would be agreeing with me that you need sun. Annie won't mind. She knows I do things differently."

"Aye, that you do, but it's not you lying here in front of God and all of creation."

"I'll lie next to you. That way I can cover you with the blanket if I hear her coming."

I lay next to him for the better part of an hour. He closed his eyes, his head lying on folded arms. I lay on my side looking at him. Maybe Annie was right. Maybe it was providence.

Scooting opened up a whole new world for the both of us. William was able to go outside with me every day and keep me company as I worked in the garden. I even persuaded him to help me weed a little, although I had to keep reminding him not to be too zealous. He would pull up everything in sight.

"Take only the weeds," I instructed.

"Which are the weeds?"

"Well, I guess the ones that aren't the cabbage."

For me, there really were no such things as weeds. They were all special in their own way. I have been told by the American herbalists here that sweet dandelion is considered a weed where they come from and that people go to great lengths to eradicate them. Imagine! My dancing, humming dandelions. Well, it just goes to show that you turn almost anything into something bad, something evil. Dandelions are weeds and healers are witches. Imagine.

CHAPTER 11

I was called that night to care for a young lad in the village. I didn't have to wake William to tell him I was going. He woke as I dressed.

"How long will you be?" he asked.

I hated leaving him, even for a short while. It must have been unbearably lonely for him, lying for hours not knowing when I would return.

"I don't know. I hope not long. I will leave you pottage and water on the stool, next to the bed. Don't try to move." I gave him a stern look.

He smiled. "I won't move."

"Promise?"

"Promise."

I gathered my things, tucked my herbs into my plaid, and kissed him on top of the head. It had become our ritual, my pecks on his head, like a mother to her bairn.

I walked toward the village with no moonlight and very few nighttime sounds. It was almost eerily quiet. The father had not called for me, as usually happened, but rather a neighbor, a woman. She knew little of the child's illness, a fever with rattles in the chest was all she had said. I had brought some of the herbs I knew to be helpful with lungs—dropwort, lungwort, rue, coltsfoot, and heart o' the earth, but I wouldn't know what was needed until I could see the child. As healers, we all have our ghosts and nightmares. For many midwives, it was having a baby's head out with shoulders not coming. Some healers were scared of bleeds or burns. For me, it was lungs. I never felt so helpless as watching a child struggling for breath, eyes wild with fear, arms flailing. I had a foreboding about this night, but didn't know if it was a true premonition or just my fear presenting itself. Whichever, I dreaded what was to come.

The cottage was dark and smoky. The older children were huddled in the corner, quiet with fear. The mother was past the point of panic, an ominous sign. The father sat with his back to the child's bed, eyes averted, never once glancing in my direction. I addressed the mother. How long had this been going on? What was the progression of the illness? What remedies had they tried? It all boiled down to one horrible fact—the child had been ill for days and they delayed in calling me. I sat with the lad for hours, trying this potion and that. But, in the end, it was just that— random attempts, too few and too late. Even as the wailing of the mother and children filled the home, the father never turned toward his son, never turned his face toward me. There was no discussion of payment. I left, dusk falling, for home.

The cottage was dark. I hated leaving William without a candle, but the thought of a stray spark sending the whole place up in flames with William stranded in it had kept me from it.

"William." I spoke into the darkness, making my way to the candle on the table. No reply. "William," I said again, panic in my voice. I lit the candle and carried it to the bed. He was lying there, awake, staring into the darkness. I leaned over to help him to sit, legs dangling over the side of the bed.

"Why didn't you answer me? I was worried." I moved the uneaten pottage from the stool and sat next to the bed.

"Worried about *what?*" The anger in his voice caught me by surprise. "I should think that if you can leave without a thought of me, you would have no cause to be worried now."

"I didn't leave you without a thought, William. You know that. It took longer than I thought. I'm sorry."

"I'm the one who is sorry. I'm sorry I was ever left here, in your way, obviously a burden. But, you agreed to care for me. You're not holding up your end of the agreement. You can't just leave me lying here whenever you see fit. I could starve to death or …"

"Agreement?" I struggled to keep my voice even. "You were dumped here, on my bed, a filthy, stinking pile of rags. I didn't agree. I was given no choice. Your brother didn't give you a backward glance, just left."

I walked to the hearth and stoked the fire to heat a pan for eggs. I picked up four eggs, two in each hand, and continued ranting. "Do you think I wanted a cripple to care for, day in and day out? Do you think it has been easy, cleaning you, turning you, waking all night to check on you, make sure you are breathing and alive?" I placed three of the eggs on the table and cracked one into the pan. It sizzled as it hit the hot iron. "What do you expect me to do? Sit in this cabin with you and never go out?" I paused in my tirade to draw a breath and turn the egg.

William said nothing. I continued. "As for starving to death, you obviously have enough strength left to yell at me. You're not too weak for that."

A sob came in my throat. I had not cried for years and was not planning on doing it then, not in front of William. Instead, I picked up one of the remaining eggs and threw it at him. I must admit I had quite good aim for one who had never thrown anything at anyone in her life—it hit him squarely in the chest. He started, his green eyes wide, and then lifted his arm to deflect the next one from hitting him in the face. Dinner was rapidly becoming scarce—there was only one egg left. I picked it up off the table. William covered his face with both arms this time, but I held the egg in my hand and crushed it between my fingers. Tears stung in the corners of my eyes. The slipperiness of the egg white running down my arm made me sad somehow. The tears were escaping now and sliding down my cheeks, dripping like the egg down my arm. I sat at the table and buried my face in my hands, egg and all.

William still had not said anything. He watched me for a moment. I don't know if he could tell I was crying. I hid my face and cried silently, without shaking or sobs.

"I'm sorry," he said finally. "I was scared."

He waited, maybe to see if I would respond. When I said nothing, he continued. "I was fine at first, but then I started thinking. What would happen to me if you never came back? No one even knows I'm here, except for Annie and my brother. Who knows when Annie would stop in next? And I'm sure you've figured out by now that my brother is not coming back."

He looked down at his hands, and then ran one hand over the egg dripping off his sleeve. I wet a cloth and went to him.

"Don't you know I've thought of that?" I said softly, as I wiped the front of his tunic, his sleeve, his arm. "Don't you know that all I have thought about since you came is you, how to care for you, your wound, your sores, your legs? Since that first night when I slept with my head on the bed, next to you, to make sure you were still breathing, I've thought of little else."

I gave up trying to clean him. I was just making a larger mess, leaving him with egg smeared all over the front of a wet tunic. I raised his arms and removed the tunic, rummaged in the trunk and handed him a dry one. He pulled it over his head.

"Give me the cloth," he said and taking it, he wiped my hands and my face without saying a word.

I put the only remaining egg on a plate and handed it to him. He held it, but didn't eat.

"I've already talked to Annie. She knows everything. Well, not everything. She still believes that you're my husband, William. But, she knows about your legs, that you can't walk. We've already arranged it. She comes by on the path everyday. If she can see me, or hears us talking, if she knows I'm here, then she doesn't stop. If it's quiet, she's to check on you."

"How long had this been going on?"

"A few weeks."

William shook his head and then said, "Then why didn't she stop today?"

"I don't know. I hope she is not ill." I am ashamed now at these words. Annie had agreed to watch out for William without a moment's hesitation. It never occurred to me that she might need someone to check on her once in a while.

William picked up the plate and stabbed the egg with the fork. It was inedible—burned and impossible to chew. He bravely took a bite anyway.

"How is the boy?" he asked, choking down the bite.

"He died."

William put the plate down. "Oh, I'm so sorry." He reached his arms out toward me, a gesture that would have been accompanied by his moving to me, putting his arms around me, if he had been able to walk. As it were, he held them out for a moment and then let them drop limply to his side.

My tears welled again. "They didn't call for me in time. The husband wouldn't even look at me. I think the mother would have called sooner, but the man was afraid."

"Afraid of what?"

"They think we are witches. That I am a witch."

"Who? Who would think such a thing?"

I looked at him in disbelief. "Everyone. People. Many people. Where have you been? Have you not seen the burnings?"

He shook his head slowly. "No. No, I haven't. I've heard tell of trials and executions, but not where I come from."

"Well, it's happening here. It's why I left my village. Isobel, my teacher, was accused and burned. It was not safe to stay."

"I thought you left to follow William."

"It was not safe for either of us. We decided together."

"Was she guilty?"

"Who?"

"Isobel. Was she a witch?"

How to answer that question? Isobel was my first, my only teacher. She decided that I needed to learn the healing craft when she would find me, time after time, in the hills and woods, sitting still among the flowers. I was almost eleven years old at the time. She was the first woman, really the first person, who took any interest in me since the death of my mother. I had my moon cycle for the first time that year. I had no idea what was happening to me, although I had an idea that it was part of the path to becoming a woman. I devised a garment of linen and moss to catch the blood, but was still terrified of being discovered, of my womanhood being found out. I would hide each month in the woods, returning at night to the cottage to sleep. My father was furious, but I bore his anger without comment. Better anger than shame flung at me.

Isobel found me during one of those times. She was not a maternal woman, not nurturing in any sense of the word. I often wondered later how she had been called into healing, as she seemed to lack the tenderness necessary. But, she was a good healer, a practical healer. She told me about my cycles, assured me that I was normal, and set about teaching me her craft. I had spent so many hours with my plants that I knew them personally. They were friends whose personalities I could describe in great detail, their quirks, their habits. But, what I couldn't do was put a name to any of them. I knew them, but I didn't know *about* them. Isobel taught me their names, their properties, the best time to harvest. She taught me how to dry them by hanging them upside down in bundles, how to steep them into infusions, and work them into salves and oils.

Not a patient teacher, she would often scold me for mistakes, but she could have beaten me half to death with a stick and I would have been thrilled. For the first time in my life, I knew who I was. I had a purpose. We were very different, Isobel and I. I still look over my shoulder to see if she's watching when I do things differently than she taught me. For her, there was only one way and that was Isobel's way. But, I learned to love her and showed it in the only way I knew how. I worked hard for her, did everything she told me to, and never complained.

Years later, when she was accused, when they took her away, I betrayed her. Not directly, perhaps, but a betrayal in my heart, which is the worst kind. Isobel was a good healer, but she had a sharp tongue and a short temper. It was only a matter of time before her tongue would get her into trouble. When she didn't see eye to eye with someone, which was often, she was capable of spouting the most venomous language I have ever heard. Was she a witch? She had smeddum, more than most. She definitely flung curses about when her temper flared, but never used her healing for ill. And I know she didn't run about with the Devil, copulating and such. Even the Devil himself couldn't have borne the brunt of her temper. I'm sure he would have sent her back as soon as she laid into him.

How then did I betray her? I closed my eyes. I didn't speak up for her, didn't visit her when she was held, being pricked and walked. I closed my eyes. I didn't even have the courage to attend the execution. I hid in the woods that day, but could see the smoke. And through it all, she never betrayed me. She never named me, even under torture. My reputation was sullied, of course, through association with her, but she didn't name me. I might have been safe there, in my village, had it not been for William's leaving. Then it was time to flee.

So, was she a witch? Was I? I looked at William, wanting to tell him everything, but not daring to. "I don't know," was all I said.

"Well, even if she was a witch, what does that have to do with you?"

"Naught. But, in the end, that won't matter. When you are accused of being a witch, everything will be held against you. Things you did, like heal a child, or things you didn't do, like fail to heal a child. If you ever said anything against anyone, that will be held against you. When your neighbor's cow dies or his crops fail, that will be used against you, too. Then, if that is not enough, they will torture you until you confess with your own tongue of all of the awful crimes you have committed against God."

It is still ironic to me that, under the law, a woman held the same status as a child, her words had no significance. That is, until a confession was extracted from her and then her words were beyond question, proof positive that she was a witch.

"What kind of crimes?" William asked.

"Oh, you know, the normal run-of-the-mill witch crimes. Cursing folk and copulating with the Devil." I wiped away a few escaped tears with my sleeve. "I have never seen the meikle man. I'm not even sure he exists. But, if he does, I definitely have no interest in copulating with him. They say his member is as cold as ice, not very tempting."

"You'd think he would have warmed it up some with all that copulating," William joked. His eyes were definitely crinkly. I smiled in spite of myself.

I got us both ready for bed. As I was extinguishing the candle, William spoke.

"So, Annie's been spying on us?"

I laughed. "I don't know if you could call it spying."

"Aye, spying. And she's very good. We should send her out against the English."

I laughed again. "She'd talk them to death, that's what she'd do."

William smiled. "Most likely. Still, she's a good spy. And a good friend. You're lucky to have found her."

CHAPTER 12

It was luck, to be exact, that brought me to Annie, though I'm sure she would credit providence. I had walked for several days, not knowing where to go, but knowing that anywhere away from where I was would be better, safer. I had brought only those things I could carry easily—Isobel's small chest with her herbs and mallet inside, and a linen bag packed with some clothing, mine as well as some of William's. I tucked as much food as I could manage into my plaid, but by the time I reached the path outside Annie's house, the food had long since been eaten and I had no idea where the next morsel would be found.

I avoided walking through the village. The last thing I wanted was to draw attention to myself, so I skirted around, keeping to the hills. I then found my way back to the path, the small village visible below. I took a bend in the path and was startled to happen upon Annie's cottage. Actually, my start came less from the cottage itself and more from the din that was emanating from it. Annie's children came by their boisterousness honestly—it was passed down to them from their mother. The sheer volume the four (or five?) of them created always astonished me, but at first it downright terrified me. I had the impulse to look around, to make sure no one was looking, as I was sure their rowdiness would advertise my presence. Any neighbors within earshot must have been inured to the noise, for it did not draw reaction from any quarter. I stood on the path, transfixed by the ruckus and wondering how many children it would take to create that impressive a volume, when one of the children, a lad of about five, barreled out of the house as if being chased by the Devil himself. He was followed by two older children, a lad and a lass. The younger boy looked up as he neared the path and caught sight of me. He stopped in his tracks, causing the other two to run him clean over, knocking him to the dirt. He began to bawl, which brought Annie from the house.

"What are you young 'uns doin'? Haven't I told you not to torment your brother?"

The older two looked at me, wide-eyed and curious.

"Who's she?" the older boy asked, lifting a finger in my direction.

"Don't ye be pointing at her. It's not polite. Get in the house, all of ya." Annie nodded in the direction of the house, keeping her gaze on me the entire time.

The children scuttled into the cottage, slamming the door soundly behind them. A second later, it opened a crack and three little faces lined up, one over the other, peering at the strange woman standing on their path.

"I didn't mean to alarm you," I began, not knowing anything more profound to say.

"I'm not alarmed. Just wondering who ye are."

"I'm Mancy." This didn't fully answer her question, but I again found myself at a loss for words.

"Well, Mancy, I'm Annie. Annie Boyd. Pleased to meet you."

And with that introduction, I became a part of Annie's life and she a part of mine, even though I had no inkling of how connected we one day would be.

I explained my story to her, at least parts of it, ending with leaving my home village to find my husband. She listened attentively and then said simply, "You must be starving. Come in for a bite and a rest."

While we ate, she chatted steadily, filling me in on the goings-on in her village in amazing detail: how many families lived nearby, the names and ages of their children, which husbands drank too much. She evidently even kept up with the ins and outs of the livestock—I learned Auld Maggie's cow had stopped giving milk for no apparent reason. I tried at first to follow the thread of her narrative, but soon the whirlwind of names and details overwhelmed me and I listened with half an ear, unable to keep up with her exuberance.

She at last drew a breath. I knew no good way to ask the question, so I simply blurted it out. "I need work. Maybe I can help you here? With the children."

Annie stared at me.

"Or chores."

No response, just an amused grin.

"I don't need to be paid in coin. Food and a place to sleep would be fine."

Annie's grin widened. "Oh, lass, we can scarcely feed the mouths we have. You wouldn't ever get a full belly in this house."

I had expected that response, but was totally taken aback by her calling me "lass"—I was at least ten years her senior, if not more. I had not been addressed so affectionately in a long time. William was not prone to using endearments. He was always tender in his actions, but not his words. Isobel had yelled at me more than not, and I certainly never expected kind words from my father. It touched me that someone who had just met me only moments earlier would address me in such a familiar way. Of course, later, I realized that Annie never met a stranger and that she gave her heart totally and completely to anyone who had need of it. It must have been clear to her from the beginning that I was one of those in need.

Annie raised one eyebrow as she continued. "Of course, you might try up the path at Auld Maggie's place. Her son's away, gone to the Americas, a few months ago maybe. She's getting on in years. She might like some help. She has a tight fist, mind you, and a sharp tongue, but you could handle it, I'll wager."

She was right. A sharp tongue I was used to. Isobel had thickened my skin over the years I was with her. At that point, a tight fist didn't matter much either. Beggars can't be choosers, as Isobel always said. If I could earn my keep, that would be enough.

Annie walked me up the path to Auld Maggie's cottage. We had to knock several times before a high-pitched voice called, "I'm coming. Patience."

Auld Maggie, a thin, frail woman with a pinched face, was of an indiscernible age. In those days, even the easiest of existences could age a woman, and a hard life—well, that added years beyond measure. She must be well into her crone years, but beyond that … She didn't seem to be in poor health to me in the slightest, other than moving slowly and bent, as if life weighed heavily on her shoulders.

"Maggie, this is Mancy. She is looking for a position. She'd be able to help you out in the house." Annie spoke these words at top volume, as if Maggie were not only old, but also deaf and dull-witted. Annie's normal speaking voice was louder than most, and this amplified version resonated through the small cottage, practically echoing off the rafters.

Maggie snorted—she obviously was neither slow nor hard of hearing. She turned to examine me. Nothing escaped her notice. She took in my worn and dusty dress, my linen bag, and wooden chest. I felt she could see through me to the desperation of my heart and the emptiness of my stomach. She would have the upper hand in these negotiations.

"Room and board only. She'll work in the garden, clean the house and cook. She'll have to sleep on a pallet. I've only the one bed."

Annie looked at me and I nodded. Beggars can't be choosers. So began my association with one of the meanest women that God ever put on this green earth. But, I had a place to sleep and a roof over my head, and food in my stomach. It was enough for the time being.

My life with Maggie gave me very little time to dwell on the past—or the future, for that matter—and no time at all for self-pity. I began my chores before sunrise, stoking the fire, collecting eggs from her henhouse, and then cooking her breakfast. The morning was spent tending the garden, when the weather permitted, and then the mid-day meal. I spent the afternoon cleaning, washing linens, airing the heather bed, scrubbing the floors. I gathered peat when needed, and when possible extended my forays into the hills to look for some of my healing plants, which I sorted and dried on the sly, away from Maggie's eyes.

The only thing I refused to do was to venture into the village for shopping. I drew the line at that. Maggie was furious with me, but was pacified with Annie's offer to do our shopping for us, bringing back meat and ale, and having loads of wood or peat sent up the path when the supply was low. On those days, Annie would drop off our purchases and then sit with me outside in the garden, or watch while I chopped wood, supplying me with an endless stream of narration about her day in the village. She never offered to help me as I worked, but the background noise of her chatter helped break up the monotony of my day and made everything go a little faster while she was there.

Eventually she would sigh, pick herself up, slapping the dust off her skirt. "The young 'uns are waiting for their meal. I reckon I should head home 'ere they burn down the place."

And with another sigh, she would trudge down the path, giving me one last wave as she rounded the bend toward her home.

Those were the only days I had another human talk to me, for I was convinced before long that Maggie didn't fall into that category. I had never met anyone so spiteful and bitter in my life. My own father was a cruel man, but I had always thought that drink and the disappointment of an unforgiving life had exacerbated that—I did have a few sweet memories, before my mother died, of my father laughing and teasing her, and pulling her down onto his lap. These memories were few and far between, but instilled in me the idea that he wasn't all bad, that maybe at some point he had been a decent man. Of course, Isobel had a sharp tongue, but there was a nugget of tenderness in her heart that belied her harsh words and rough exterior.

Maggie, on the other hand, was just plain mean. I could do nothing to satisfy her. If I cleaned, it was still dirty. If I cooked, it was tasteless and spoiled. I bathed her with water that was too cold and I was rough in my touch. If I had said the sky was blue and the grass was green, she would have argued that I was not only dull-witted, but also colorblind.

I somehow understood that her dissatisfaction with me had more to do with her own miserable life than my competence in the kitchen. I spent time while I was working in the garden, or chopping wood, creating in my mind her story, the one that led her to such an unhappy place. I invented for her a horrible childhood, with a vicious mother and absent father. Her mother forced her to marry a much older man, who drank continually and beat her just as regularly, while she mourned the unrequited love of her life, a childhood friend, who was killed in a farming accident. She had her own children die in her arms, and her only friend steal her husband from her, leaving her penniless.

But, in reality, she wasn't penniless—she had stashed away more than a few coins in a jar hidden at the head of her mattress. And I knew from Annie that at least one son had not perished in her arms, but lived in the Americas, which Annie figured was as far as he could get away from Maggie's brutal temper. So, as my imaginings unraveled, I was forced to concede that Maggie was, as I said before, just plain mean.

Not that it mattered much. I wasn't expecting kindness. I noticed her harsh words, but it was as if I heard them from a distance. By the time they reached my ears, they had lost their sting. By that point, the sweet hope of happiness that we are all blessed with at birth had been chipped away through my life—sometimes coming off in huge chunks, but mostly sliver by sliver—leaving me hollow inside. Hollow and hardened, like an old tree struck by lightning. Maggie's spiteful words simply rolled around inside me, but there was nothing soft and tender for them to wound…

CHAPTER 13

So, our days went. The unrelenting work kept me from dwelling on my past and on what tragedies had yet to befall me, for that is how I perceived the course my future would run. I suppose we would have continued that way indefinitely, if it were not for the unusually short summer, even by Scottish standards, that led to an early, particularly harsh winter.

It caught us unaware—we had all expected at least a few more weeks of sunshine and mild days. We were actually in good shape for the winter. I had diligently built our wood and peat supply, and we had a goodly amount of grains stored in wooden casks under the table. Maggie's little jar of coins was the most comforting winter provision I could think of. I had never had more than two coins to rub together most of my life, so her nest egg seemed like a fortune. My only fear of a long winter was being cloistered away with Maggie for months on end. Annie would come when she could, but I dreaded those lonely days when even a trip to the woodpile would be an adventure.

I was selfish in those fears of loneliness, for the winter had much worse to offer Maggie. I had never seen such a rapid decline. It was as though her body had needed those expected weeks of daylight and warmth to set in its stores for the winter. When she was slighted them, she lost her footing. And was unable to regain it.

A rattle set in her chest with the very first cold snap. Thank goodness I had stolen every possible opportunity away from my chores to gather some plants for the winter. I still had what was left in Isobel's bags and I had managed to dry more through the summer spent with Maggie. For the first time since I had left my home, my skills as a healer were called for, and as reluctant as I was to establish a reputation in this new village, I was unable to sit by and watch her struggle for breath.

Even through bouts of congestion and fevers, she was feisty to the end. She would fight off a cold of the head, only to have it settle in her lungs. She would fight that off as well, cursing me and the fever and her children, scarcely able to draw breath.

It took it out of her, though. Her words remained sharp, but her body weakened and became frail. I turned her and cleaned her, but her skin was thin as worn linen and the bedsores finally overtook us both. They covered much of her body and I tended them as I knew how, with my salve of comfrey. I searched her body every day for signs of new sores, but overlooked the back of her head, the ones that were covered by her hair. By the time I noticed them, it was too late.

I should have known it was her last day, for it was the first time she ever called me by name.

"Mancy. Lass."

"Tell me, Maggie."

"He'll not come back."

"Who, Maggie? Who'll not come back?"

"My boy, my son. He'll not come back. I don't know why he went so far away. I don't know why he hated me so much." She struggled for a breath. "No matter. You'll stay here."

"I'm not going anywhere. I'll stay as long as you need me."

"After. You'll stay. Use the coins. I don't remember what I was putting them away for. There are more hidden in the hearth, behind the loose stone."

She closed her eyes and turned her head away from me. Then, she turned back suddenly, eyes open, wide and frightened. "Don't leave me, Mancy."

"I'm here, Maggie."

I crawled into the bed with her and held her in my arms. All of a sudden, I was holding Lizzie again, her breath hot against my face. Maggie was my baby, my mother, my love. I stroked her hair and sang her my wordless songs. I fell in love with her at that moment, all of her spite and harsh words forgotten. How does that happen so quickly? Why doesn't it happen more often? I sat with her body long after she drew her last. It was so quiet with her gone.

We buried her at the Kirk. I figured she'd be furious at that— she hated the church—but it was the proper thing to do. Annie had spread the rumor in the village that a niece had moved in with Maggie, to tend to her, so no one questioned my presence at her funeral. And nobody seemed to even notice when I returned to the cottage and made it my home.

CHAPTER 14

I had almost nodded off to sleep that night when William spoke. "Mancy, I've been thinking."

"That's good. Thinking is good," I said sleepily.

"Seriously, I've been thinking about William. Your William."

"What have you thought about him?" I was awake now.

"What if he comes back and here you are, sleeping in the bed with a man who has stolen his name."

"Well, to be truthful, I stole his name and gave it to you."

"I don't think he will care how it came to me. A man would not be happy about it either way."

I paused. "He's not coming back."

"How do you know? It's been a long while, but he could be looking for you right now. It's only a matter of time before he finds you."

"He's not coming back."

"You can't know that."

"Yes, I can. I know that, because I buried him."

Silence. I turned on my side to face him. There was a small hole in the front of his shirt and I touched it with my index finger, worrying it this way and that. I didn't look at him.

"What happened?"

"The village where we lived—there was an illness, many

children died and old people, too. Our daughter Lizzie—Elizabeth—died from it. She was five."

"I thought there were no children."

"There aren't now, are there? She was our only one. There were two babies, boys, but they didn't live out the day. She was our only one."

"What was the illness?"

"In the lungs. It took so many, so quickly. I had been tending all over the village, mostly children. Very few lived."

"And William?"

I continued playing with the hole in his shirt. It was unraveling while I spoke. "We buried Lizzie at the Kirk. William died less than a week later. I did everything I knew to do. Isobel was already gone—they had burned her weeks before—so I was on my own. Nothing worked."

"I don't understand then. Why say he is gone away? It is no shame to bury a husband."

"You're right—you don't understand. How could you? You can't know how frightened I was. The women who were being accused and burned—most of them were alone, widows. And, I was already being talked about. Isobel was my teacher, everyone knew that. I knew I had to leave, so I made up a story. William had left for work and I would follow."

"So," William was putting the pieces together, "when you say you buried him?"

"I mean *I* buried him. By myself. That night."

"You buried a grown man, dug the grave? It usually takes two strong men for that."

"Aye, it was harder than I thought. I buried him under the woodpile, so if the grave was not deep enough, at least the wood might keep the animals out. The problem was, then, I had to keep the grave from extending out from under the wood. I couldn't let anyone find out."

William said nothing.

"The problem was William had stacked it tall, rather than long or wide."

He contemplated this, looking at me all the while. I kept my gaze on the hole, which was now large enough to admit my entire finger.

"What did you do, Mancy?"

What had I done? First, I had lain with the body for several hours. I had seen death many times before. I knew the sound of that final breath, the slackness of the jaw. Still, I lay with him, just to be sure. While I held him, I devised my plan. No one could know of his death. The talk stirring after Isobel's execution would be increased now that so many under my care had died. It mattered not that my own daughter had died. A rational person would say, "See? It is not her fault. She could not even save her own." But, what was said, instead, was, "See? Only a witch would kill her own blood." Now, to have lost my husband also. The plan was simple. I would bury him under the woodpile. I would tell the neighbors that he had gone to the city for work. The crops had done poorly enough the last few years that it was not unthinkable he would do so. I would wait one week, gather my things, and flee.

I pulled him off the bed, holding him under the arms, much as I did to move William, the other William. His heels thudded against the floor as they flopped off the bed. An awful sound. I dragged him to the woodpile, which luckily was not far, just outside the door. As I said, it was stacked high and it took a long time for me to move it all to the side. Working with William's spade, I dug for most of the night. I managed to dig to a depth that I thought would suffice, but I knew I would never get it long enough before the sunrise.

So, what did I do? I had helped Isobel remove a leg before. A man had been injured in the fields and did not have it cared for properly and in no time the leg was black and rotting. This could not be so bad as that. That man had screamed and struggled even with whiskey in him and several men holding him. William would not protest, would not even notice. I took the ax from the woodpile and marked a spot on his leg, more than halfway up, but far from his groin. I made myself see a piece of wood instead of his leg and swung hard. I didn't want to have to do it more than once or twice on each side. I then rolled him into the grave, put his legs on top of him, retched over it all, and began to replace the dirt. I stopped after the first few shovelfuls, and ran back into the cottage. His flute was lying on the table, waiting to be buried with its owner. I placed it gently under his hands in the grave and began covering again. By morning, the wood was back in a neat pile and all that was left to do was to clean the last few hours off of my body.

I didn't tell William all of this, the details. He understood with one statement.

"I had removed a leg before."

My finger stopped fussing with the hole. I could feel his skin, his chest, and I stroked it slightly. I couldn't even imagine what he must think of me. It seemed more horrific to me now, reliving it through William's eyes. What he must think of me.

My breath stopped and I could feel myself slipping away, as I used to, into nothingness. But then, he placed his hand on my hair, at the nape of my neck, brought me back and pulled me close into him, my face buried in his chest. I fell asleep in his arms.

CHAPTER 15

Villiam brought up the idea not long after I told him about my husband's death. We were sitting out on the hill, our favorite spot, next to the garden. I had been weeding here and there, and picked some cabbage for a soup. He was supposed to be helping me, but kept fiddling with the same clump of weeds for minutes on end, winding them around his fingers instead of yanking them up properly. When he finally spoke, he didn't beat around the bush.

"Mancy."

"Mmm." I had given up on the garden and was lying back on the grass, my arm over my eyes.

"I think you should marry me."

If I'd been surprised by my first proposal of marriage, I was absolutely stunned by this one. I didn't say anything, didn't move my arm away from my face. I don't even know if he was looking at me when he said it. As with so many moments, I have had to fill in the details in my mind.

"Mancy. Did you hear me?"

I sat up slowly and brushed the grass off the back of my dress. I was wearing a dress that day for some reason, I don't remember why. Maybe it was wash day and everything else was hanging out to dry. I just remember brushing off the back of my dress, and pressing my apron flat with my hands. William leaned over and picked a piece of grass out of my hair, which had fallen loose as I was lying back.

"We already are married. You know that."

"I mean for real. Not just in our minds."

My head was spinning. I had never once asked William about his life, where he came from, what he had left behind. I had been living in a false world for so long, that I had almost forgotten there was a different reality than the one I had created. I told myself it was better not to clutter the picture with unnecessary facts, but truth be known, I had grown attached to the idea that he was my husband, and didn't want to know if another was waiting for him, missing him.

"What would it serve, William? We couldn't do it in the Kirk—as far as everyone knows, you're already my husband."

"We'll do it by contract."

"Why not leave well enough alone?"

"Because it's not well enough. It's just a lie."

"My whole life is a lie, William. You should know that by now."

We were face to face now. I searched those green eyes for some clue as to what this all meant. He was staring at me just as intently. For the first time in my life, I felt as if someone knew me, could see me, all of me, inside and out, good and bad. I wanted to tell him everything in that moment, my secrets and my nightmares, my hopes and desires.

Instead, my question came out as a whisper. "Why would you want to marry me, William?"

The moment I asked it, I wished it were back in my mouth. I didn't expect a declaration of love and didn't want him to think I did.

He held my gaze for a second longer, then shook his head slightly and looked away. "I might to able to offer you protection, if we are married."

I tucked a strand of hair behind my ear. Protection. It was close to love, if not the same. "I have one question."

He looked up quickly. "I'll answer you anything."

"Are you free to make this offer?"

He smiled, eyes crinkling. "I wouldn't make it otherwise."

"There is not another then?"

"No, no other."

"Very well. I accept."

William smiled and pulled himself up straighter, running his hands through his hair. "Ready?"

"Here? Now?"

"Where else would you have it done?"

"I don't know. Inside would be more proper, don't you think? And a witness. Don't we need a witness?"

"Who were you thinking of? Annie? Do you want it spread around the village that we are just now getting around to getting married?"

I smiled. No, Annie was out of the question.

He continued. "You don't have to have a witness. We can both declare our intentions and that will stand. And inside might be more proper, but out here on the hill suits you better. You don't belong inside."

He was right as usual. He scooted closer to me and took my hand in his.

"Wait."

"What's wrong?"

"I don't even know your true name."

William smiled. "That's easily remedied. My name's—"

"Wait."

"Now what?"

"Don't tell me. Let's leave it be."

"Sure?"

I nodded. "Aye, I'm sure."

So, there on the hill, next to the cabbages and kale, we stated our intentions. I married him without even knowing his true name.

I realized later that I was right that day. He did know me, better than anybody had or ever would again. But, what he didn't see, what I had managed to hide away from him without even knowing it, was how much I loved him and how much I wanted him to love me in return. I doubt that I knew it myself.

CHAPTER 16

Ioften wondered when it was that William fell in love with me.
I know, for myself, it was a gradual process, but only because
I would not allow it any room to grow, no air or sunshine to
bloom. It probably started from the first night I cared for him,
but I refused to acknowledge it, especially to myself. It is a sad
fate when you begin believing your own lies. And when, later, I
felt myself caring for him more than I imagined possible, I would
stifle it once again by saying to myself, "It is only on your side.
He does not care for you." Not until the night that we made the
salves did I allow myself to believe that he might return those
feelings.

It all started with those stubborn bedsores. I had done
everything I could think of to heal them—salves, poultices,
turning him, putting him in the sun. They would get better, just
long enough for me to draw a deep breath, then here would
come one and then another. The truth was that a body was not
intended to lie in bed all day and bedsores were a testament of
that fact. I finally decided on a course of action. What William
needed was a better bed, a softer mattress. We slept on a mattress
of heather, which was actually quite comfortable, but I got it into
my head that if I could put him on a feather mattress, all would
be well.

A poor healer didn't just run off to market to buy a feather mattress. I was sure they were quite dear in price. But, I hadn't forgotten the pouch behind the stone in the hearth. I had not intended to use it, mainly out of stubbornness and spite toward his brother, but ridding William of the bedsores would certainly be a worthy use of the money. I hesitated for another reason. Turning up in the village with a pouch full of coins to buy a feather mattress would set tongues a wagging and draw attention to me. I thought of asking Annie to make the purchase for me, but if there was to be talk, it would be of me, not Annie.

I set out one morning, the day of the salves, for the village. I didn't tell William what I was doing, just that I would return soon and would be bringing a surprise. I tried to remove the pouch without his noticing, but have since realized that William noticed almost everything.

I left at first light. My plan was to find a mattress and pay to have it brought up the hill to the cottage. I had also hoped to find beeswax and oil. I needed the beeswax to replenish my stock of comfrey salve, as I had used almost all I had on the bedsores. If I could find a decent oil, I would make an infusion of lavender, as well. Lavender was not a plant I could find on my hills. It was Annie who had first brought it to me, several months ago. She came into my garden one morning where I was working, wearing a sly grin.

"What are you up to?" I asked her. She sidled up to me, grinning widely now.

"I have something for you. Something you're going to like."

"What then?" I was growing impatient with the game. Once more, Annie was gifting my life with something special, and as usual, I failed to recognize it.

She pulled a linen bag from her plaid and handed it to me. "Smell," she said. I opened the bag, although that was unnecessary as the fragrance of the lavender seeped through the linen and had already reached my nostrils.

"Oh!" I had never smelled anything so sweet, so pungent, yet delicate. "Oh!" I repeated.

Annie was practically quivering with excitement. Her smile would have broken a less sturdy face. I knew I wouldn't have to ask her how she came about this find, for she was already bursting to tell me.

"You remember when I found you that oil from that gypsy peddler, you know, the almond oil. He asked what I needed it for and I told him you were a healer making salves." I winced inwardly at Annie's total lack of discretion, but said nothing. She continued, "He was back in the village. I stopped by to see what he had new. He remembered me and told me he had something you would like. It was this—lavender, he calls it. He says the fragrance is used by brides to calm their nerves and entice their husbands. He said you should put it into the oil he sold you last time."

Why in the world she would think I would need a fragrance such as this? I was not a bride and did not even have a husband at the moment. But, I had to admit that the smell instilled in me a sense of peace.

"How much do I owe for it?"

"Oh, nothing really. You can give us some barley or oats, when you are next paid."

Later that day, I infused the lavender into the oil, as the peddler had suggested. It was an amazing thing, that scent. I took to using it when I went to heal, not on the patient, but on my hands. I had the idea that the smell would calm the patient, and that they would associate my care, my touch with something beautiful and delicate, rather than the pain and trauma of the illness I was tending. If nothing else, it calmed me and I often used it at home, when I was lonely and in need of something to soothe me.

I never told anyone about what happened in the village that morning I went to buy the mattress. Not Annie, not William. I hadn't wanted to worry them. My own life was so full of worry already—surely a little more wouldn't matter. I convinced myself that the talk was just that. And I knew that even if it weren't idle chatter, there was no help for it. In my experience, there never was.

CHAPTER 17

I made sure William was set up for the morning before I left. As I trudged down the path toward the village, I realized that it was the first time I had entered the village on my own, without being beckoned by a distraught family member or nervous father. I practiced in my mind what I would say—"I need a mattress." "Do you know where I can find a mattress?" "A feather mattress." "Aye, a mattress."

As I walked, I realized that I had no idea where to find a feather mattress. They existed—of that I was sure. Not in my life, of course, but in fine homes. But, where to find one? Still uncertain, I continued toward the village.

The inn was on the outskirts of the village. I had been called there once by the wife—she couldn't conceive. I sat with her for several hours, asking her about her life, her desires. We were interrupted by the shouts of her husband. She had not told him that she had turned to me for counsel. He threw me out into the street with no payment for my efforts. What he wasn't aware of was that our meetings continued—she came to my cottage every day for a month. She couldn't pay me, but she brought me food from the inn. She paid daily in food for my sense of smell.

I had always possessed a supernaturally keen sense of smell. I didn't realize that it was different from others' sense of smell,

until I began my studies with Isobel. I could identify the dried
herbs by smell, as in their dried form they often favor each other
too much to tell them apart otherwise. Isobel would rely on my
ability to tell one from the other, if they had become jumbled
in her bag. But, I also developed the ability to detect illnesses
by their smell, something Isobel never taught me. Stomach
ailments smelled sour or metallic. Lung ailments smelled musty.
Liver disorders smelled like vinegar. There was a distinct smell
right before the birth of a baby, right before the mother began
to push. I never mentioned this to Isobel. She did not like me to
learn things outside of her guidance, even if I stumbled upon
discoveries on my own.

The most practical aspect of my sense of smell was the
ability to detect a woman's ripeness. I noticed it on myself first.
Of course, there is a smell associated with a woman's moon, with
the fresh blood, but a different smell comes with her fertility each
month. As a young girl, I didn't understand the ramifications of
the different smells of my cycle. No one had bothered to explain
the details of human reproduction to me—that was something
William was left to teach me. But, after I married, I realized that I
could identify my fertile days, not only by physical sensations, but
also by smell. Of course, on myself, I was most aware of the smell
that emanated from between my legs. Later, as I tended more
women who were in their childbearing season, I could detect it
just as easily on their breath.

You must understand that this information meant a great
deal to many women, who either wanted nothing more than to
conceive a child, or nothing more than to not. I could visit a
woman in her cottage and with one whiff, tell her whether she
should entice her husband that evening, or give him too much
ale and work on the mending until he was snoring. It was that
simple. Of course, nothing in the world is foolproof. The one
drawback was that a fertile smell was accompanied by increased
desire, so that even a woman who had decided not to add
another mouth to feed at that time would often forget the logical
reasoning behind her decision and find her resolve crumbling,
when faced with a most willing and ready husband. Those who

succumbed would often come to me later for a different sort of assistance. There were, of course, herbs used to bring on a cycle, but I always thought it much simpler to prevent the pregnancy in the first place.

With the innkeeper's wife, my thought—my hope—was that I could pinpoint her fertile days by smelling her every day for a month. Or two. But, it was of no use, as she had no discernible change in her odor. I had never met another woman whose odor didn't change at all. She did have a smell particular to her—the scents of the food and ale from the inn hung on her clothing. But, underneath, nothing.

I looked into the darkness of the inn. The wife was sweeping the floor. She looked up as I passed. I almost lifted my hand in greeting, but decided against it when I saw her eyes. Her eyes wouldn't let me lift my hand. They were empty, just as her womb was. In that moment, I understood why she would never carry a child. It wasn't her fault. She had been drained of all life by her husband. He had left her womb empty and her eyes empty and her heart empty. I wished I had been able to understand that earlier, but it wouldn't have mattered. He was her husband and he had drained her and there was nothing I could have done to change that.

I decided that the first stop I would make would be at the market where Annie bartered and bargained for me. I hoped the gypsy peddler would be there. I needed oil anyway and I thought he might be able to direct me toward a mattress. I wondered if I would recognize him, but needn't have worried. I knew him immediately.

"Pardon me."

The gypsy lifted his head. He smiled. "You are pardoned. How may I help you?"

"Um, I'm not certain. My friend, Annie, usually does this for me. Do you know Annie? She is a large woman. Loud. She likes to laugh…"

The gypsy had dropped his wares from his hands and was looking at me with an open mouth. He grabbed my right hand in both of his and bowed low over it. I thought he was going to kiss it, but instead he touched my hand to his forehead and held it there.

"You are the one she has told me about." He lifted his head just enough to look at me, but held my hand firm. "It is such an honor to meet you. An honor and a pleasure."

I looked over my shoulder to see if someone had walked up behind me. Someone who deserved such words. But, it seemed he was addressing only me. "You are Mancy."

I nodded. He had bowed his head low over my hand again. He had the blackest hair I had ever seen. Black and curly. But, not like any curls I had seen, not like William's loose loops that fell over his ears and wound around my fingers. Gypsy curls were twisted so tight that they formed a shiny, smooth surface. I reached out with my other hand to see if it was softer than it looked, but I couldn't bring myself to touch him.

"It is fine to touch." He spoke without lifting his head. "I don't mind."

I shook my head and managed to extricate my right hand from his grasp. "I just need some oils. And a mattress. But, I don't imagine you have a mattress." I looked behind him as I spoke, hoping a mattress might materialize suddenly.

He laughed. "No, no mattress. Oils, I have plenty of. But, let's not rush. I have wished to meet you for a long time."

"Me? Why me?"

"Because you are special. You have special gifts. Some would say magical powers."

"Oh, no. Not magic. I just do what I do. What I know how to do."

"Things that no one else can do. That is magical, don't you think?"

Magic? That was a bad as witchcraft in these hills. A woman could get stuffed into a barrel for less that that. "No. Just what I know how to do."

He tilted his head and smiled again. "Come. Sit for a moment. I want to tell you things."

"What kind of things?"

"Many things. I am like you, in a way. You talk to plants, animals, babies that aren't yet born, no? I see things. Things as they are and sometimes things that are yet to be. It is what *I* know how to do."

"You want to read my palm? Tell my fortune?"

He laughed, exposing a mouthful of white teeth. "Is that what you expect of me? Reading palms? No, that is for gypsies and fools."

"But, that is what you are, isn't it? A gypsy, I mean, not a fool."

"Who told you that?'

"Annie. She calls you the gypsy peddler."

"Many call me that, I suppose. But, that is not what I am. Do I look like a gypsy to you?"

I had only seen gypsies once in the village I grew up in. They had come through with their wagons loaded with goods and children. My father told me not to look as the wagons passed so they would not be able to place a curse on my head. I had looked, of course. They were dark-skinned with shiny black hair. They didn't seem dangerous—just weary and maybe a little bit afraid themselves. In fact, I wondered if the gypsy parents had told their children the same thing my father told me, because the little ones kept their faces hidden behind their mothers' skirts as they passed through.

The peddler who wasn't a gypsy took my hand again and led me behind his wagon. He had a small room set up there with chairs, a table and a pallet on the ground, all covered by the side of the wagon that was lifted to form a roof, supported by carved wooden poles on the four corners.

"Please, sit. Would you like some tea?'

I shook my head.

"You won't mind if I have some?"

I shook my head again. He busied himself with the fire.

"Well? You didn't answer my question. Do I look like a gypsy to you?"

"Well, aye, you do. But, then I have only seen gypsies once and didn't get a good peek because my father told me not to look. But, they had dark hair, like yours."

"As do many, many other people in this world. Spaniards, Moors, the Hindus. And many others."

"And you?"

"And I am from Venice. In Italy."

I nodded, even though I had never heard of such a place. "So, you are ..."

"A Jew. A Venetian Jew. Do you know of the Jews?"

I shook my head. I knew of the English and the Gaelic-speaking Highlanders and gypsies. I knew many Scots were leaving for the Americas to find their fortunes, or least steady employ. But, I knew nothing of Jews.

"Have you not read the stories of Moses and Abraham in the Holy Book? Or, had someone read them to you? Maybe in church?"

"I don't go to Kirk often." An understatement, if ever there was one. I had never attended as a child—my father refused to step foot in the place. William had gone every week when we were married, but I almost always found an excuse not to attend—a baby on the way or weeds to pull in the garden. And since coming here—well, I had gone exactly once. To bury Maggie.

The peddler was searching through a pile of books that were stored in the interior of his wagon. "If only we had more time. I could read you marvelous stories."

"About Jews?"

"About Jews and Gentiles and Chinamen and the natives of the deep dark of Africa. So many stories. But, that will have to wait. Now, I will tell you a story about you."

"About me?"

"Yes." The peddler held in his hands the book he had extracted from his pile. It was leather-bound and had an engraved circular symbol on the front. He placed it on the table in front of him and held the palm of one hand over it, without touching. He closed his eyes and reached his other hand out to me and, without touching, held it in front of my face. For the first time, I caught his scent and had William not been waiting for me, helpless and alone, I would have been hard-pressed not to pack my few belongings and follow him to Venice or the ends of the earth. He smelled of herbs that were unlike any found in the Scottish hills. And he smelled of books, like the one lain out in front of him. And he smelled of oils and perfumes and sadness. All mixed together, wafting toward me from the palm of his hand.

His eyes still closed, he smiled and began speaking to me in a soft, melodious voice. "Your mind is strong. You have much knowledge."

"No, I never had schooling. My father didn't believe in schooling children. Especially not a girl. I can't even read."

He shook his head. "Not that kind of knowledge. A deeper knowledge. You know the earth, her plants, her creatures. You know smells and sounds. Anyone can learn to read, but your knowledge came with you into this world. And you will pass it onto your daughter."

I shook my head. My sweet Elizabeth would never have the opportunity to receive such a gift. I started to explain this to him, but he was already speaking again, slowly lowering his hand to my throat. "Your voice is blocked. Your words won't come. But, your heart is strong. Bruised, but strong." He shook his head. "A pity."

"What's a pity?" The heart or the bruising?

"It's taken. By another. I was going to ask you to come with me, but it's not to be."

I was beginning to think I would have fared better with a palm-reading gypsy. This Jew had missed the mark again. "There is no one. I am alone."

He shrugged and continued. "Your pain is in your stomach. Someone has wounded you there. That is where you keep your fear. But, it can be healed. Nothing so bad that it can't be fixed."

His hand continued its journey downward until he almost

touched my feet. He opened his eyes. "Well, what did you think of my story?"

"Is that all?"

"Mostly. Some of it is for you alone. You will learn that part of the story later. On your own. But, it is a good story, yes? Strong mind and strong heart. Open your throat and when you do, the pain in your stomach will go. Then, you will be whole again."

"What about you?"

"What do you mean? What about me? Do you have a story to tell me?"

"No, no story. It's just that I smell things on people."

"And what do you smell on me?"

The world, I wanted to say. Oils and perfumes and books, I wanted to say. "Sadness," I said.

"Sadness. Yes, of course, you would smell that. Let's just say that it is not always easy being a Jew in this world. There was a great sickness in my city, which took from me most of my family. Evil took the rest of them. I had a business, a wife, children. And now, I have my wagon and my stories and I live my life as a gypsy. It is not a bad life. I come to your country with the warmth of summer and travel back when the winter winds come."

"Back to Venice?"

"No, never back to Venice. Many places, but not Venice."

"Will you come back next year?"

"Of course—how else would you have the oils and lavender you need to do what you know how to do?" He filled my jars with oils and refused my offer of payment. I tucked them in my plaid and extended my hand. He took it in his two and bowed low again. This time, I reached out and touched the softness of his tight curls.

"When you come, I will make you an ointment. To wash the sadness from your hands."

"I look forward to that, Mancy."

I turned to leave, but remembered my original task. "Where do you think I might find a mattress?"

"Hmm. I would try the tailor's shop. A mattress begins with the cloth and stitching, no?"

I nodded. "Of course. A good thought. Thank you...." I still didn't know his name.

"Moshe."

"Thank you, Moshe."

CHAPTER 18

The tailor shop was on the far side of the village, past the Kirk and the graveyard where Maggie was buried. I glanced toward her grave as I passed, but no amount of money could have enticed me to stop and pay my respects properly. Instead, I whispered a greeting to her as I hurried on to the tailor's shop. I knew the family that owned the shop, having attended the birth of their youngest not too many months earlier. The labor was fast and intense and I had watched with surprise as Agnes, the tailor's wife, had transformed from a quiet, almost meek, being into a wild beast, caged against its will. She paced back and forth across the small bedroom during her pains, bellowing. Her husband stood at the far wall, watching her pace. Each time she reached the wall where he stood, she would snort at him, head tilted and nostrils flared before turning on her heel for another round. She neared him again, but this time she laid her head on his chest, nuzzling the exposed skin at the base of this throat. I smiled at this tender display of affection, especially since I had been concerned that she was going to rip his head off a few minutes earlier. When the pain overtook her though, all tenderness disappeared and she bit him—hard—at the base of the throat. He didn't flinch. I could see the half-moons of tooth marks, already turning blue, as she resumed her pacing. I wondered if I should say something about not mortally injuring one's husband during labor, but in the next instant she was pushing and the baby slipped into my hands. Later, when Agnes was tucked into her bed, quiet and meek once again, I rubbed chickweed salve on his wound. I was curious to know if this same transformation had overtaken her during her other labors, but wasn't sure how to frame the question.

"Agnes really, um, is not herself during childbirth?"

"Oh, no. That'll be her. She was better this time, though. She only bit me once!"

I was smiling with this memory as I stepped into the shop. Agnes had always been kind to me, so her reception on this day took me aback. "Mancy! What in the world are you doing here? I don't remember calling for you."

"You didn't. I came on my own."

"Is that wise? Coming to town on your own?"

I gave a little laugh. "I didn't know coming to town required wisdom. I thought two legs were enough for the trip."

She didn't laugh. She glanced around and then pulled me by the arm to the back of the shop. "It's just that there is talk. About you. There are rumors of a man in your cottage—that you have sickened him to keep him captive." She glanced around again and lowered her voice. "Annie says he is your husband, but no one believes that. And you—you never come to town, you never talk to people. You have no friends. It is not normal for a woman to live on her own like that. They say you are, well, not an ordinary woman."

I thought about Moshe and how he had said the exact same thing about me, but when he said it, I felt as though he had given me wings. Now I was back where I belonged, back in the dungeon.

"Who has been saying these things?"

"Who hasn't? You know how people are. When one talks, the rest join in. I have told them that you are fine, just quiet and solitary. I told them you helped me when I needed you—that you have helped many of us when we have called. But, that is

not good gristle for the gossip mill. You should be careful. I don't
know if you're hiding a man up there in your cottage or not, but
you should take care. It wouldn't take much for the whole village
to turn against you."

Agnes lowered her voice. "There's more." She dragged
me deeper into the store. "Thomas Campbell is saying you are
responsible for the death of his son and wife."

"Who?"

"Thomas Campbell. His wife gave birth a few weeks ago.
She died. So did the bairn."

I shook my head. "That wasn't me. He has the wrong
midwife. I haven't lost a bairn or a mother. He must be confused."

"No, he means you. He says he couldn't call for you because
you are a witch and that he had to attend to his wife himself. He
holds you at fault."

I didn't want to ask the next question, but it came out
anyway. "What happened? At the birth?"

Agnes continued in a whisper. "Well, I wasn't there myself,
of course—this comes from Annie, but it might have a kernel
of truth to it. She says the head came out but the shoulders
stuck. Thomas pulled and pulled until there was no use pulling
anymore. He told his woman to stand up and walk outside—he
was going to cut the baby out with a knife. When she stood, the
baby fell right out on the floor—dead as could be. And, after the
baby came a river of blood that just wouldn't stop. Poor woman
didn't stand a chance."

I closed my eyes. "Agnes, you know I had naught to do with
that. I could have helped if he had called, but he didn't! How
can he blame me? I don't even know him!"

"Aye, you do. Don't you remember? You tended his wife a
few months back. Remember? The one with bruises all over her
face. You tended her and told him to stop beating his wife. That's
the one—Thomas Campbell."

That one. I hadn't even asked for a name. I just wanted to
finish my work and leave as quickly as possible. "Still, how can
he blame me for this? It doesn't make sense!"

Agnes shrugged. "Sense? It has naught to do with sense! Says you placed a hex on him and his family. My reasoning is that he messed it all up so badly that he had to blame somebody. Might as well be the village witch."

Witch! That's what they were calling me. So, Moshe was wrong. I wouldn't be healed and whole. It sounded so easy when he said it. But, he was no gypsy and he wasn't very good at telling fortunes.

Ignoring the lump in my stomach, I forced myself to focus on the task at hand. Witch or no witch, I refused to be deterred from my quest. "Agnes, I need a favor."

"What kind of favor?"

"I need a mattress. A feather mattress. The gypsy told me I might find one here. It is very important."

"And what is wrong with a heather mattress? Are you too fine to sleep on the heather anymore?"

"No, it's not that. I can't explain. But, it is important."

Agnes sighed. "I can make you one. But, they are expensive. How would you pay for it?"

"I have money. I can pay. Can I take it today?"

"Today?" She laughed. "Not even next week. I have many orders to be filled before you and a mattress takes time. I can sew the outer casing, but you would have to find the feathers for stuffing. And that will cost even more."

More than a week to wait. And then feathers to be found. What had I been thinking? That I would stroll into the village and leave with a feather mattress on my back? Yes, that had been my plan and it was now in shambles.

"Agnes. I have money. I need a mattress now—today. I can't explain to you why, but it is essential. Is there anyplace in town— anyone that you know—that might sell me a mattress?"

Agnes lowered her voice again. "I made a mattress several months ago, in the winter, for the minister's wife. She had been ill for some time and he thought it might help her be more comfortable. She passed on last month. I don't know what he has done with her things, but you might see if he still has the mattress. But, Mancy, be careful. He will not be pleased to see you. He talks about you as well. About how you don't attend Kirk. About how you are godless, or worse. I suggested he call for you when his wife worsened, but he refused. Said that those who do not do the work of the Lord must be doing the work of the Devil. He even mentioned you from the pulpit. Not by name, mind you, but we all knew it was you."

"Why hasn't Annie told me this? She has said nothing."

"Annie? She can't hear the sermon for snoring. If we sit close enough to her, neither can I. I am surprised she doesn't chide the minister for interrupting her nap. Besides, even if she were to hear it, she wouldn't think it was you he was ranting about. She adores you—in her eyes, you can do no wrong. She is almost like a proud mother bragging on her bairn—Mancy can do this and Mancy can do that. Can't shut her up sometimes."

"Do you think I do the Devil's work, Agnes?"

"Me? No, lass. But, it doesn't matter what I think. In the end, the ones who hold the power have the final say. I can sew a straight seam, but the minister pieces together bigger things— thoughts and ideas and words that can save you or damn you. Don't underestimate him. And don't flash that money of yours around. They're already saying you've made a pact with the Devil. If they see you flashing a sack of coins, it'll be the proof they want."

"I'll be careful. Thank you, Agnes. And thank you for trying to defend me."

"You're welcome, lass. But, I'm afraid my defense will do you no good in the long run. I'm just a tailor's wife. No one listens to me."

CHAPTER 19

The minister's home was across the cemetery from the Kirk. It was the finest house in the village, with a heavy front door and several stories. The fence that surrounded the graveyard extended to enclose the front yard of the house, where there was a small garden that had been taken over by weeds. I pushed through the black rod-iron gate and resisted the temptation to spend a few minutes freeing the poor garden of the intruders that were strangling it. Instead, I walked straight to the front door and knocked with my fist. The door was so heavy that my pounding scarcely resonated, so I tried again, using the brass doorknocker this time. I jumped a little—the doorknocker created a much louder sound than I anticipated and for a moment I considered bolting back past the sad garden and through the gate toward the safety of my cottage. But, I decided that I had come this far and it would be cowardly of me to flee just because I was afraid of a doorknocker. I stood back from the door, smoothed my dress and waited.

A young woman opened the door. I wasn't sure whether she was the maid or perhaps the minister's daughter. I tried to remember whether the minister and his wife had been blessed with children, but couldn't pull to my mind any details that I might have heard.

"Is the minister at home?"

The lass said nothing but left the door ajar and scurried into the dark of the house. Unsure whether I was expected to follow, I stepped part way through the open door and waited. When I heard footsteps approaching, a lump rose in my throat and I made my way back out the door, off the stoop and waited in the yard, near the garden.

The minister's eyes widened when he saw me. I must have interrupted a meal, because he had a napkin tucked into his collar. He removed the napkin and used it to wipe his thin lips and then blew his nose.

"Aye? What is it that you want?" He didn't wait for my response. "I must say you are the last person I expected to be standing at my door. Quite a nerve, have you? Gall, even."

I shook my head. Nerve? Moshe hadn't mentioned anything about my nerve. Or gall. Probably because I didn't have any.

"Agnes—I mean the tailor's wife said that you might have a mattress for sale. A feather mattress. That belonged to your wife?"

"I know who it belonged to." Spittle formed in the corner of his mouth as he spoke. "But, it is not for sale. You couldn't afford it anyway. And there is nothing you have that is worth bartering for. Unlike some of the ill-informed folk in this village, I do not value your services." He spat in the yard and began to shut the door.

"I don't need to barter. I have money." I held up the brown bag, but remembering Agnes' words, tucked it quickly back into my plaid. "I can pay."

"How did you come upon that much money? I know you can't have earned it. Perhaps you made a deal for it?"

So, he thought I had struck a bargain with the Devil. I smiled, thinking of William's brother. He certainly had plenty of the Devil in him.

"You have no reason to smile. None. As a matter of fact, I would wager that you will have little to smile about for the rest of your days. God does not bless those whom He counts among His enemies."

I am not His enemy, I wanted to say. But, Moshe was right—

my throat was blocked and the words wouldn't come. I turned to leave, but couldn't tolerate leaving without a mattress, so I made a final attempt.

"You can think what you like of me. But, you have a mattress that belonged to a dead woman and, unless I am very wrong, it is sitting there in the room she died in, unused and untouched. I have money. It is none of your business how I came by it, but I promise you that it was by honest means. So, you can keep the mattress until *you* die or you can sell it to me. Your choice. Oh, and your garden is choking from all the weeds. It needs attention." I stopped as I uttered these words—at that moment, I knew how his wife had died. She had choked, been strangulated, from the inside out. A disease that twisted her insides and wound its way through her spirit, slowly suffocating her. I wouldn't have been able to do anything for her, even if he had called me. I felt a wave of pity for him—it must have been unbearable watching her suffer like that.

"By the way, I am sorry for your loss. I know how hard it is to lose someone you love."

He pinched the bridge of his nose with his thumb and forefinger. But, then he waved his hand at me. "I don't need your sympathy. Take it. Take the mattress—I don't want your tainted money. Just take the mattress and be gone."

"I'll send a lad for it. This afternoon."

"So be it."

I dropped back by the tailor's and arranged for Agnes' eldest to carry the mattress up the hill for me. I paid him well and gave him some extra to leave at the minister's house—I wanted no charity from that man. I finished my shopping quickly, swinging back through the market on the way home. I looked for Moshe, but the spot where his cart had been was empty and I wondered if I had dreamed him up. I had conjured things in my mind before. But, his smell was still on my hands and he stayed on my mind all the way home.

CHAPTER 20

I splurged on a special meal for us, mutton and some ale. William never complained about the scarcity of food or lack of variety, but surely he was accustomed to a much heartier diet than the one we were living on. I couldn't have cared less about what I ate, so long as it kept me alive, but I often worried that he would starve to death eating like this, a bite here and there. With a few other purchases—some new candles, and twine for drying my herbs—I headed back for the cottage. Amazingly enough, there were still coins jingling in the pouch. I hadn't spent it all.

The mattress had not yet been delivered when I arrived back at the cottage with my bundles, so William assumed the surprise I had alluded to was the food and ale. I said nothing to dissuade him from that notion, but was so excited that I reminded myself of Annie with the lavender, grinning like crazy.

"What are you so happy about?" William asked.

"Nothing. Do I have to have a reason to be happy?"

"No, it's just that I have never seen you smile this many times in one day, let alone in one hour. What are you up to?"

"You'll see. Now, it's outside to tend the garden and chickens. We'll have a good dinner and I'll show you how to make a salve tonight."

We spent the rest of the afternoon outside. I worked in the

garden and collected eggs, and William watched me from his blanket. Not long before dusk, the lad from the village came up the path, toting the mattress on his back. I had him put it inside on the bed, over the mattress of heather. William waited until he left, then worked his way down the hill and into the cottage.

"A new mattress," he said.

"Aye, of feathers. For your bedsores."

"Help me up then, to try it out." I lifted him on the stool and from there onto the bed.

William lay back. "It's nice." He was doing his best to sound unimpressed, but he smiled as he spoke.

"Nice? Is that the most you can say? I spent all morning looking for that mattress." I was doing *my* best to sound annoyed, but was smiling all the while as well.

"Well then, come on up. Give it a try." I climbed up next to him and we lay there, on our backs, surveying the rafters. It was heavenly, the softness of the down, the way we sank into it, the way it wrapped around us.

William finally spoke. "It won't work."

"What do you mean? You don't like it?"

"No, I mean it won't work. It will defeat your purpose of ridding me of bedsores, for I will never move again. I plan to stay in this bed forever."

"Well, you have to get up at least once more, for we are to have a proper dinner tonight and then you have promised to help me with the salves. I need you to pound the beeswax."

"Once more, then. For dinner and pounding beeswax. But that will be the last time."

"All right. Once more." Neither of us made any attempt to move, however.

As we lay there, I became aware of his breathing, deep and regular. We lay so quietly I imagined I could hear his heart beating. And floating over us both were the smells.

Since William, the first William, had left, I didn't notice my change of smells anymore. Indeed, my cycles had stretched out to almost nothing. I didn't know if it was because of my age, or if my body knew there was no use in wasting its energy on fertility. Whatever the reason, my body had decided that fortunes had changed, that there might be some use for fertility after all. My smells had returned with a vengeance, as had my cycles. Thinking about it now, it makes sense. My body had no way of knowing that my proximity at night to William was just that, a sharing of space. No, it was too busy absorbing the new presence of masculinity to notice much of anything else. For just as women release odors, so do men, only theirs is constant and unrelenting.

Since that first night, when William arrived stinking so badly that I had to bury his breeches, I had been aware of his smell. My husband William had a mild smell that was never overpowering even when he was drenched in sweat. It never offended me, but then it also never compelled me. This William had a stronger, earthier smell. At first, I thought it was that he was exuding all of the herbs I had been pouring into him, but later realized that it was just him. It filled up my cottage to the point that it was the first sensory acknowledgment of arriving home. I have never found a word to put to that smell. Musky, yes, but not really. Strong, but not overpowering. The best way to describe it is that it was the masculine equivalent to lavender, not that any such herb exists. If it did, I would be the first to bottle it, infuse it into oil, and put it into a salve. I loved that smell.

I reluctantly decided that the salve was not going to make itself, and managed to convince William to give up the mattress long enough for dinner at the table. We took our time eating, chatting, laughing. I had not had ale for quite some time, and it did not take much to make my head light. William told me stories of his childhood and his home. As he spoke, I realized that he had grown up in a grand house, with many rooms and fireplaces large enough to stand in. For the first time, I saw my life—the dark of the cottage, the roughly hewn furniture, my worn clothing—through his eyes. For the first time, I was ashamed of who I was. I opened my mouth to apologize, to beg his forgiveness for I don't know what.

William took a bite of the mutton and sighed. "This might very well be the best dinner I have ever had."

I shook my head. "I'm sure you've had finer."

"Finer? Maybe. But, not better. This is better than any meal I remember."

I laughed. "That's just because I've been starving you for some time now. I could have cooked you your own boots and you probably wouldn't have complained."

William smiled. "No. It's not that. It's much more than that. It's everything. Waiting for you to come home from the village, wondering what you were up to. It's working in the garden with you this afternoon. It's the mattress. It's everything. Then, sitting with you, here, eating, talking." He took a sip of ale, leaned his head back, and sighed again. "Don't you see? It's all that." He looked around the cottage. "It's all of this."

I nodded. But, I didn't see. I cleared the table of the plates and poured him some more ale. William continued his narrative, relating memories in no particular order—the early ones while his mother was alive and later ones of the adventures his brother and he had in the woods, all of the trouble they stirred up. He spoke so fondly of him, I had almost convinced myself that it was a different brother he was talking about.

"Your younger brother? The one that I met?"

"Aye, my only brother."

"You were close to him."

"Aye, I was. But, over the years that changed. He changed, I think. He became ambitious, greedy. I have been in his way for a long time."

"What do you mean? In the way of what?"

"The only thing I had that he wanted—to be firstborn. I think it drove him mad. It was the one thing he couldn't manipulate in his favor. That is, until now."

I didn't like to talk about his brother. It made me too painfully aware that William was only mine on loan, that he could be reclaimed at any moment.

William seemed to read my thoughts. "I doubt that he will

return at this point. I'm sure he's already told my father I am dead. I fear I will be in your care for some time."

"Don't fear on my account. I have almost become accustomed to having you around. And if you pound the beeswax for me, I will want to keep you for always. I hate pounding the beeswax."

I laid out the supplies for the salves. I had used the last of my almond oil to make an infusion of comfrey, as well as one of heart o' the earth and goldenrod. I began the process of straining the infusions through several layers of linen, while William broke up the beeswax. The chunks needed to be small enough to melt into the infusion rather quickly, so as not to overheat the oil. I had let several batches scorch when first learning and was pounded about the ears by Isobel for it. Keeping the chunks of wax small was key to not scorching the whole lot.

William worked with a small wooden mallet that I had taken from Isobel's cottage the day she was burned. I felt no guilt in helping myself to her herbs, oils, and anything I used with her in her healing. I didn't want her money, not that any would have been left after she was charged for her own execution. The wooden chest I used to store my herbs was hers, as well as the wooden mallet for breaking the wax. William used it now to pound the wax wrapped in a piece of cloth. I stopped straining the oils long enough to watch him. He worked carefully, methodically, pounding with a steady rhythm. It is tiring work—I knew that from experience— and once in awhile, he would shift the mallet from one hand to the other. I was impressed that he was equally dexterous with both. He looked to catch me watching him, and I quickly turned back to my oils.

Wax pounding was tiring, but oil straining was messy. I had pushed the sleeves on my tunic up as far as they would go and had tucked the tail into the breeches to keep it from dipping into the oil. I poured the oil from one container into another, through several squares of linen cloth. I would let all the liquid drip off and then wrap the squares around the herbs remaining on top and squeeze the rest of the oil out. Soon, my hands and arms were covered with oil and I rubbed it into my skin. I almost leaned over to rub the excess onto William's hands and arms, but stopped myself. I knew then that my feelings for him had changed, because I would not have thought twice about such an innocent gesture before.

We pounded and strained until the beeswax was in smallish chunks and the oils were free of herbs. Of all the things I learned from Isobel, making salve was my favorite. It was time-consuming, lasting two to three days if you take into consideration the time needed to infuse the herbs into the oil. Then, the wax pounding, straining, and finally, blending it all together into a salve. Using butter was much quicker, you simply added the crushed herbs into soft butter and applied it straight away. I did that when I ran out of my beeswax salve or if I needed to apply a salve over a large area, an entire leg or back. The beeswax salve was much better suited for smaller areas, a burn on the hand, or William's bedsores.

I began to heat the oil at the hearth. This was the most difficult part—melting the wax without burning the oil. I pulled William close and showed him how to add the wax, bit by bit. Too little wax made the salve thin and runny, more like a balm. Too much wax made it stiff and difficult to apply. The trick was to start with less than you thought you would need and then add slowly. I showed him how to hold the wooden spoon and use it to press the wax against the side of the pot. At first, he was too vigorous in his stirring, causing the oil to splash. I held my hand over his to help him feel through the spoon, to sense the melting of the wax. Our fingers intertwined and I could feel the wooden spoon, could feel the wax giving under our hands. The chunks of wax clinked softly against the pot as we stirred. William's scent rose with the heat of the fire, mingling with the oil rubbed into my hands and the lavender I had used earlier. I remember every detail of that moment.

We poured the first batch into small jars to cool and harden. This was the batch with the comfrey. We then returned to our respective chores of straining and pounding for the next batch of heart o' the earth and goldenrod. Over the rhythmic pounding, William began to unfold pieces of my life.

"Where did you learn how to do this?"

"From Isobel. Of course, I already knew the plants, but she taught me how to use them—how to make salves and potions and teas."

"How old were you when you started?" William always started by asking the easily answered questions first.

"Ten, maybe eleven. I had already received my first moon," I said without thinking, then blushed. He didn't seem to notice, or didn't respond if he did.

William stroked his eyebrow with his thumb. We continued in our work, and I wondered if he had satisfied his curiosity about this part of my life.

"Who taught you about the plants, then? Before you learned from Isobel."

I didn't answer immediately. No one had ever asked me about that part of my life, the nebulous years between my mother's death and Isobel's taking me on as a student. Even my husband had not ever asked me much about my early childhood. I'm sure he assumed I learned everything I knew from Isobel. If he had asked, I wouldn't have told him everything. It's not that he would have thought differently of me, but that he simply would not have understood.

"I'm not sure. I just knew."

"What do you mean?"

"I just knew. From the time I was very young, I would sit in the woods, on the hills for hours and listen."

"Listen to what?"

"The plants." How outlandish my own words sounded. Even Isobel would have never understood if I had told her that plants talked to me.

"The plants," William repeated.

"Yes, the plants." I sounded defensive.

"What did they say, Mancy?" William asked softly.

I looked up from my straining. I assumed he was making fun of me, but no. He truly wanted to know.

I told him everything. At first, I thought I was hearing my

mother's voice, because the plants had sweet gentle voices, like hers. They would comfort me, a child grieving for her mother. They would sing to me, without words. I spent as many hours as possible sitting amongst them, learning to listen. In return, I asked them who they were, what they did. I learned to hear their answers in my own body. I could feel a burning or swelling in my heart, my lungs, my gut, and I would know what part of the body they were to help. Looking back, they were my best friends, my only friends. I'm sure many people would think they were the imaginings of a lonely little lass, but they were not of my imagination. They were of my heart.

I busied myself with the oils as I told this to William. I was scared to look at him, scared of his reaction.

Finally, he spoke. "Maybe you truly are a witch," was all he said.

The oils began to spin in front of my eyes. I held the edge of the table to steady myself. What a fool I was for telling him my secrets! "Maybe you truly are a witch." Of course, that was my fear, my deepest fear, that despite all of the lies, I could not deny the legacy that was rightfully mine. Perhaps, I truly was a witch. Of all the people who would eventually say those words about me, William was the only one who wounded me. I forced myself to look at him, to receive the full force of his words, his accusation.

But, he had returned his attention to his task of pounding the wax. He was smiling, slightly, eyes crinkling. His was not the face of accusation. On the contrary, it reminded me of the look on my husband's face when I was shy during lovemaking. He would tease me, but his smile told me that he was pleased with me.

I began my straining again, but then walked to the basin of water, in which I had soaked some fresh flowers earlier in the day—bluebottles and dandelions. Without saying a word, I picked up the basin and dumped it unceremoniously over William's head.

He gasped from the cold, water running down his face and

chest, flowers in his hair. "What are you *doing*, woman? Trying to drown me?" he sputtered, as he wiped water from his face and brushed stems and leaves off the front of his shirt.

"You'll be more careful who you call a witch next time." I wanted to be angry with him, but couldn't help but laugh at the sight of him, soaking wet, bluebottles and dandelions everywhere. "Here," I said, untucking the hem of my tunic for him to wipe his face on.

He dried his face on the fabric, while I picked blue and yellow flowers from his hair. Then, instead of dropping the hem of the tunic, he took me at the waist with both of his hands and buried his face in my middle. His hands, amazingly large, almost reached around me, even though I was not slight in build. His fingers pressed on my back and his thumbs rested under my lower ribs. At first, the top of his head was against my stomach, but then he rolled his head upward, and I could feel the outline of his face through the thin cloth of the tunic—his brow against my rib cage, the outline of his nose, and the moist heat of his breath, in and out, on my belly. He pulled me closer to him, and I could then feel his lips, as well. It reminded me of a baby I had delivered that had decided to enter the world face first. The bag of waters had not broken and was over its face as it began to emerge. I could feel the outline of its nose and mouth through the membranes. As I touched it, the mouth began to root for my finger, through the bag. I imagined touching William's face through the thin linen of my tunic, his eyes, nose, and mouth, rooting against my fingers.

He didn't move for several seconds. I held my breath, keeping my hands out to both sides, unsure where to put them. I wanted to put them on his head, to stroke his hair and pull him up to me, but some invisible force stopped me. Finally, I laid my hands on his shoulders. I was trembling.

He still didn't move. I slowly became aware of a sound that at first I thought to be crying. But, he didn't seem to be crying, his shoulders were steady, not shaking. No, the sound was more of a sniffing. He was inhaling my scent, his nose rooting rather than his mouth, against my tunic that had been splattered with infused oil and lavender, and underneath, my own scent of ripeness, which was so strong that even an ordinary sense of smell would have been unable to ignore it.

"Your smell—" he started, but I pulled away and returned to the business of straining the oil. We finished our work in silence, putting away several more jars of salve to harden. I helped him change into a dry shirt, and put him into bed for the night.

"Are you coming to bed?" he asked.

"No, I need to clean first. Go to sleep." I stayed awake for most of the night, waiting until he was breathing regularly and deeply before crawling into bed beside him.

I wish now I had been willing to accept his desire for me that night. I will always regret the time I wasted.

CHAPTER 21

I smelled the mustiness before I heard the rattle in his chest. He had a cough for a few days that I had been paying attention to. I brewed an infusion of heart o' of the earth and was giving it to him several times a day. Forcing would actually be a more accurate word, because, unlike his acceptance of my brews when he was unconscious, he was acutely aware of the taste now. He complained with every sip.

"How much more of this vile brew must I take?" Sip. "It is really awful." Sip. "I'm not sick, you know, just a slight cough." Sip.

Finally, I had enough. "It was one of my vile brews that kept you alive, so stop your moaning and drink. A slight cough can lead to much worse quickly, you should know that. I swear, you're worse than a child with all your complaining."

He didn't complain anymore, at least not with words. Instead, he made faces, contorted as if he were being tortured, with each sip. I had to laugh, something I found myself doing more than I ever had in all my years put together. Even during those few years that I was truly happy, in my first years of marriage and after Lizzie was born, I didn't laugh much. I didn't know how.

As I reached over him to retrieve the empty cup, I smelled it, that staleness of congestion in the lungs. Without saying a word, I pulled up his shirt and put my ear to his chest and then his back. A definite rattle. A panic rose in my heart—I hadn't tended his wound, legs, and bedsores just to have him succumb to congestion in the lungs. His lack of activity was partly to blame. Just as the legs are meant to move, the lungs are meant to breathe deeply with walking in the fresh air and working hard in the fields. William had managed to keep his arms strong by scooting around the yard and in the garden, but he had no activity beyond that. I listened again to his back. The rales were loose at least, not tight and high-pitched. If I could keep them loose, so he could cough up the phlegm, maybe it would not worsen.

Although my logical mind was caught up in the panic that was washing over me, my hands and heart were able to feel what needed to be done. I would bake it out of him in the sunshine. We went on the slope next to the garden, where he usually rested and watched me work. I spread out a blanket and had him lie on his stomach, over my lap, his shirt off. Using my fists, I pounded his back, up and down, on either side of his spine. He tried talking to me as I worked on him, but soon gave up. Instead, I sang to him, my songs without words, pounding on his back in time to the song. Rhythmic and meditative movements. After I had pounded sufficiently, I sat him up, his back in front of me. Using the oil infused with lavender, I rubbed it into his back, up and down, following the path of the pounding. Then I used both hands on either side of his spine, and traced the outline of his ribcage. I worked on the muscles of his shoulders, which were tight with knots, probably from having to use his arms and shoulders to scoot around with. I worked down from the shoulders to the shoulder blades, working out the sore spots on either side.

What had begun as an effort to bake the rattles out of his lungs with the heat of the sun had turned into an exploration of his body, his muscles and bones and skin. I used the strength of my hands to work out not only the knots and kinks, but to work out my fear and loneliness, my grief and loss. I worked my way up—back, shoulders, neck, scalp. He was melting into me as I went, so that as I massaged the oil into his hair, he ended up leaning back onto me. I rubbed over the front of his shoulders, onto his chest, and finished with my hand resting on his heart, much as I had done when he had first come to me. We sat for a long while, silent. His heart beat under my fingers. Still alive. He covered my hand with his.

I closed my eyes and lifted my face to the sun. Even with my eyes closed, I could see the brightness of the rays. I could feel its warmth on my cheeks as well as the warmth of William against me, and I could feel the oil on his body, under my fingers and soaking through my tunic. There are some days in life that belong in a jar, to be put on a shelf for later. I desperately needed this day later, but then there was no jar, just the imprint in my mind. It was so indelibly imprinted, however, so brilliantly and clearly, that it will be many thousands of years before I forget it.

It seems funny to me now that I fought so hard against him, loving him, needing him. There on the hillside, in the sunshine, his hand over mine, it seemed easy, as natural as the breaths we were taking together in time.

It seemed an eternity had passed when William spoke. "Could you ever love a man with no legs?"

"I already do."

I leaned him up away from me a bit and then helped him lie back onto the blanket. I lay next to him, my body touching his, my legs covering his. I kissed him, his face, his mouth, his eyes. Then using my fingers, I began the journey from healer to William's lover, using my touch not to discern illness or divine remedies, but to pour into him, into every cell of his body, my love for him, a love unlike any I had ever experienced before.

CHAPTER 22

That night, I lay on William's chest as he ran his hands up and down my back, tracing the outline of my spine with his fingertips. His hands ventured lower and he planted them firmly on my backside. He kissed me.

"We should go to sleep."

"Aye, we should." I waited. "I'll blow the candle out." William didn't move. "Which I'll do as soon as you let me go."

William shook his head. "I can't." He pulled my hips closer into his body. "See, I can't let go. I've been snared. I'm thinking you must be a kelpie."

"A kelpie? A slimy loch monster?"

"Aye, but disguised as a beautiful woman. Or a horse. They say once you touch her, you can't let go. And she'll drag you down into the depths of hell. One lad even cut off his hand to get away."

"So, which am I? Beautiful woman or horse? Be very careful how you answer. It wouldn't be wise to anger the kelpie."

"Well, it's hard to say. I've seen some fine horses in my day." He hesitated, eyes crinkling. "And some beautiful women, too. I'd be hard pressed to choose one over the other."

"To the depths of hell with you, then. Or do you want to cut off your hands? I could help with that, need be. Don't forget,

I've taken off limbs before." I tried to sound angry, but ended up laughing, slapping him on his head and chest.

He shielded his face from my blows, protesting, laughing, and finally taking my face between his hands. He stared at me, his green eyes soft.

"You have ensnared me."

I held his gaze for as long as I could, but then pulled away from him to blow out the candle. "There's no such thing as kelpies anyway."

William sighed in the darkness. "You're sure of that?"

"Aye. Have you ever seen one?"

"What if I said I had? What would you say to that?"

"I'd say you're lying. I saw a dragon's eye once. It doesn't mean such creatures exist." It was my turn to sigh. "People see what they want to see. And close their eyes to that which they can't bear to see."

William patted the mattress. I climbed into the bed next to him and draped my arm lightly over his chest.

"Just because you can't see something, Mancy, doesn't mean it is not there. I've never seen God in His Heavens and He is there just the same."

I sighed again, quietly.

"Don't tell me you don't believe in God?"

I shrugged. "I used to. Remember how I told you the plants talked to me? I used to think, when I was a little girl, that it was God talking to me, telling me which plants healed burns and which ones stopped bleeding. But, it couldn't have been, could it?"

"Why not?"

"Because their God, the Kirk's God, doesn't bother himself with plants and healing. He only cares for metal."

"Metal?"

"Metal and fire, torture and pain. In His name. In payment for crimes against Him. So, it couldn't have been Him. But, sometimes, I still feel Him, when I know, almost without thinking, what I need to do to heal someone. When I know where to go to find my plants, I just go over a hill and there they are, just what I need. Those times I think maybe He's there, the God I know. But, how can that be? He can't be both, now can He? My God and theirs, at the same time. So, I think there must be none at all. He simply doesn't exist."

William stroked my hair softly. "I know He exists."

"How, William? How can you know that?"

"He gave me you, didn't He? That's all the proof I need."

In the darkness, I ran my fingers along his dark eyebrows, along the length of his nose and then traced the soft curve of his upper lip. I couldn't argue with that. Annie had been right, all those weeks ago. Providence had brought William home to me.

I had almost fallen into sleep when William brought me back with a question.

"A dragon's eye?"

CHAPTER 23

I remembered the dragon's eye from one of the first births I had attended with Isobel. It was understood that during my early days with her that I would simply observe, silently, handing Isobel whatever she needed. I was also to clean after the birth, and scrub the linens in the washtub before I left. I had successfully carried out my duties at the other births I had attended—three or four by that time, I don't remember—and I was feeling confident in my new role as midwife's apprentice.

The labor was progressing smoothly for this mother who had already borne three other children into Isobel's hands. Even as a new apprentice, I recognized the change in the mother's sounds, the catch in her throat that let us know pushing was imminent. I scurried about, as quietly as possible, getting together the supplies I thought Isobel would be asking me for—the clean linens to slip under the mother's hips, the moss to place under the linens to catch the fluids, the clean thread Isobel would use to tie the baby's cord. I turned toward the mother to prepare the bed when I was stopped dead in my tracks by the dragon's eye.

The mother was lying on her back, feet on the bed and legs falling to the sides, allowing me a full view of her most precious parts. She was pushing, softly, not with full force. Instead, with each pain, she would spread her legs further and grunt slightly.

There, at the entrance, or exit—depending on how you look at it—the bag bulged with each pain, opening her just slightly, exposing a shimmering, incandescent pearl. I looked quickly at Isobel—surely this was not normal—babies' heads were not translucent. Then I realized what I was seeing was the bag full of waters that had not yet ruptured. It created a dragon's eye, opening vertically and then winking closed when the pain was over. It was the most beautiful, eerie sight I had ever seen. I stood, clutching the birth supplies in my two hands, mouth dropped open, unable to tear my gaze away from this hypnotic eye that was opening and closing, time and again, ever so slowly. At some point, I realized that everyone in the room, except the mother, who was in the timeless realm of laboring women, was looking at me. I cut my gaze toward Isobel, still unable to turn my head away from the dragon's eye, and saw, rather than heard, that she was shouting at me, gesturing frantically for the linens and moss. I pulled myself back into reality and managed to prepare the bed, just as the dragon's eye exploded, showering both Isobel and me in the face. I sputtered and groped for my apron to wipe my face, but Isobel simply reached down, eyes blinking and fluid dripping from her nose and chin, and caught the baby that flew out behind the arc of fluid. "Ye can wipe your face after the bairn comes out," was all she said.

I had never mentioned the dragon's eye to anyone. Isobel didn't comment on it, if she had even noticed it. Maybe it was a run-of-the-mill happening for her, that she had seen hundreds of dragon's eyes in her years as a midwife. But, even after I had as many years as she had catching wee ones, I never saw the dragon's eye again.

I told William about it—the dragon's eye—that night of the kelpie. The night of mythical beings. I had to describe it to him several times, as he had never seen a baby entering the world and was not aware of such things as bags and fluid.

"Have you never seen the birth of a lamb or a calf?' I teased him. "It is just the same only different. They come out feet first, but bairns come out head down. Well, most of the time." I decided against educating him on the variety of breech presentations possible. "What I mean is that it's all the same—there's fluid and sacs and blood, no matter what kind of critter you are."

"But, how is it that it was a dragon's eye and not a cat's eye or a dog's eye?"

"Because it winked sideways. Not like this," I winked to show him, "but up and down, sideways. Like a dragon's eye."

"Well, how do you know how a dragon winks? Have you ever seen one?"

Good question. Of course, I had never seen one, but I had seen a picture of one, once in a book. It was one of Annie's precious finds at the peddler's cart, a book full of words and drawings of bizarre creatures that surely didn't exist, but had been pulled from the imaginings of who knows what kind of strange minds. Neither Annie nor I could decipher the words, but the peddler had told Annie the names of some of the creatures—dragons, griffins, chimeras. There were also pictures of witches, old hags astride brooms, naked and contorted, their faces displaying a grim pleasure from the wooden shaft between their legs. Witches I knew, of course, but not these witches. Scottish witches were different, evidently, in that they didn't use brooms as a means of transportation. Some of them were thought to sail in an upside-down eggshell, but never a broom. I saw no one I knew in the picture of the broom-straddling witch. Not Isobel, not myself. But, I did recognize the dragon's eye, the beautiful oval slit with the bulging bag of forewaters. Maybe the first person who thought up dragons had seen what I had seen, a translucent pearl between a mother's legs. But, what did the first person who thought up witches see? Isobel with the fluid dripping off her chin and nose, blinking and grimacing as she deftly caught the baby flying out? Me, mouth dropped open, entranced by the winking of the dragon's eye? Or a hag, breasts drooping, elbows and knees angular and harsh, laughing as she pulled the broom tighter into her flesh? I guess we will never know.

CHAPTER 24

The next few weeks reminded me of the first weeks I tended him—dreamlike and timeless. The first time I was adjusting to caring for him, this stranger who had been deposited into my life with no warning. This time the adjustment was one of falling in love, unabashedly and completely. I could not satisfy my need for him—his touch, his voice, his smell. Once I allowed myself to love him, I couldn't imagine that I had ever denied him in any way. But, behind the joy in loving him was a tinge of dread. The more you love something, the harder it is to lose. I don't think I ever believed he would be mine forever.

Our routine was the same as it had always been—working in the garden, tending the chickens, cooking, eating. Nighttime had not changed, either. I still put him to bed facing the left and then turned him, once onto his back, and finally onto his right side before the morning. Those three positions became my favorite part of our life together—I spent much of the day looking forward to the night. He began on his left, I on my right, my legs replacing the blanket that was folded between his legs for support. We held each other and talked until our words trailed off in mid-sentence and our eyes closed on their own accord. In the middle of the night, I would turn him onto his back, this time my legs propping his at an angle, to relieve the strain on his hips and lower back. I would snuggle in close to him and place my left hand on his chest, over his heart. Finally, before the morning, I would turn him once more, and this time I would be pressed against his back, the contours of our bodies matching, my arm around his waist. Sometimes in the night while I was turning him, he would wake and we would talk more, or make love before falling off to sleep again. Nighttime was my refuge against the possibility of losing him and the reality of my precarious position in the world.

Winter was on the way, but the summer that had been stolen the year before, when Maggie fell ill, was being returned to us in the form of mild days. I was thrilled—it meant more time in my hills, though I did not wander as far afield anymore. An invisible thread pulled me back to the cottage, to William, every time I strayed too far. Instead, William and I spent hours in the garden, which was flourishing with the sudden onslaught of attention after weeks of neglect.

It was during one of our garden afternoons that I finally was brave enough to delve into William's life, to put into words questions that had been lingering in my soul for some time.

"William?"

"Mm?"

"How is it that you never married?"

"I did marry."

I paused in my weeding to look at him.

He laughed at my expression. "You. I married you."

"That's not what I had in mind."

"I know, but it's so easy to rile you. I can't resist."

"I'm not laughing."

"Sorry," he said, but as he was still smiling, I doubted his sincerity. "I did ask someone once, a bonnie lass."

"What happened?"

"She said no."

"Why?"

He shrugged. "She didn't want me."

"She didn't want you? How could she not want you?"

He smiled. "I suppose I wasn't always the fine catch I am today."

I eyed him suspiciously. "What was wrong with you then?"

He sighed. "I was young, full of myself. I didn't understand it then, but later I saw. She didn't want me because I didn't want her, not really. I mean I wanted a beautiful woman to stand by my side. That's what I saw in her. I never really saw *her*."

"What happened?

"I was angry, furious really, but I got over it. I used to have quite a temper, but the years have worn it down, as they are wont to do." He sighed again. "She ended up marrying my brother."

"Your *brother?*"

"Aye. Of course, that fueled my anger even more. But, it made sense. He didn't take her for granted. It was the first time in our life, I think, that he beat me at something. Before that, he was always in my shadow. I was taller, more handsome, more at ease with women."

"And more modest?"

He laughed. "Well, I already told you I was full of myself. Too full. No room for a woman to fit in with my high opinion of myself. It's funny how life forces things into order, balances things."

"So, she chose him over you?" I was having trouble processing that bit of information.

"Aye, she did. I think he courted her, at first, to spite me. But, in the end, he truly loved her. I think he saw her, as I was never able to. "

"Then, she is your sister-in-law?"

"Was. She died in childbirth. So young."

"What happened?"

"She bled out. The baby died as well." He fiddled with a clump of dirt. "It about killed him, my brother."

"Since then, there have been no others? For you?"

"Nothing to speak of."

"Aye, but plenty not to speak of?"

"A few," he conceded. "But, none like you. You, you are my

first true love. You, I see. Day and night, sleeping or awake." He paused. "I see you completely."

I found myself holding my breath as he spoke. As much as I loved to hear his words, they scared me. Fate had never been kind to those who loved me. I finally forced myself to exhale. I began to breathe in time to the rhythm of my hoe, in and out with each chop. Soon, winter would come and it would no longer matter how well-tended the garden was. It would not survive a Scottish winter. Yet, I breathed—in and out—with each whack at the dirt. Futility has its purpose, at times.

William interrupted my respiratory efforts. "Mancy." He had stopped working and was regarding me with a tenderness I saw so often in him. "Thank you."

"For what, William?"

"For everything. For tending me, keeping me alive. I know I was stubborn. Hard-headed." He cocked his head toward me. "You can disagree at any point."

"Oh, no." I laughed. "So far, you're right on the mark."

William winced. "I'm so sorry."

"Really, it wasn't so bad. I've tended worse."

He shook his head. "How did you put up with me? I'm surprised you didn't toss me into a loch."

"Well, the nearest loch is quite a distance. But, I did consider the stream, once or twice."

"Why didn't you?"

"I would have had a devil of a time dragging you down there. Besides, I wanted to see your eyes."

"My eyes?"

"Aye, before you awoke I wondered what color they were. And then, after I saw them, well, they are far too green to be tossed into the stream."

"So, if they had been brown…?"

"At the bottom of the stream you would have been."

I scooted over to him and positioned myself in his lap as much as possible. He put one arm around me and leaned back on the other. He stroked my hair with his free hand.

"I'm glad they were green," I whispered.

"Aye, so am I."

CHAPTER 25

I dreamed that night that they came for me. They took me to a place that I had seen before, as in a dream within my dream. I didn't fight them, but went willingly with my hands bound in front of me. I felt surprisingly calm, with none of the panic that rises in my stomach and throat so easily in my waking moments. I couldn't see the faces of my captors, but they too seemed familiar. All of a sudden, I was a little girl standing alone in the darkness of the heavens. The only thing I could see was a woman, also bound, but she was struggling against the ropes that held her and was moaning with pain and fear. Her back was turned toward me, but someone forced her to roll over, to face me. It was my mother's face, her lips clenched tightly, as if to prevent sound from coming out of them, but not tightly enough to silence the moans that, in my dream, were not coming from her mouth but from her heart. Her eyes were wild and her hair was streaming around her face, her dark brown tresses unbound and free. I tried to scream, to call out to her, but words wouldn't come. I was mute, unable to help her, unable to save her.

I woke with a start. The familiar panic of my daylight hours hit me with full force, and I leaned over the side of the bed to retch. I was able to hit the jar, the one we kept by the bed for William's use.

William turned sleepily toward me and put his arm around me, pulling me back into the bed. "Are you ill?"

I shook my head.

"Bad dream?"

"Yes. No. I don't know." I closed my eyes and brought my mother back into view. "No, it wasn't a dream."

William moved the hair from my face, sticky with sweat and vomit. He reached over me to retrieve the cloth I kept on the stool next to the bed. He wiped my face and brow and I nestled my backside against him, pulling his arm tighter around me.

"If not a dream, then what?"

"Let's leave here."

"To where, Mancy?"

"Anywhere. Far away, the Americas, maybe."

I turned to face him now, but not looking at him, playing with the front of his tunic, as I had the night I told him about my first William. I had mended the hole, so I picked at the end of the thread that protruded there.

"That might be a tad impractical—traipsing around the globe with a man who can't walk."

"We could do it. I could figure out a way to move you—in a cart or wheelbarrow. It would be hard, aye, but we could take our time. There'd be no rush."

"But, this is home, Mancy."

"This is not home—we're living in a stolen cottage."

"It's not stolen. Just borrowed. And I didn't mean this cottage. I meant Scotland. Scotland is our home. We wouldn't be happy anywhere else."

"*Happy?* I am not looking for happiness. Happiness means nothing to me, William. I just want to survive. If I stay here, eventually, they'll find me and take me. I can't escape that. Not unless I leave altogether. Somewhere far away."

William didn't respond. I fiddled with the thread a bit longer, and then wrapped the end around my finger and snapped it off. The mending would probably unravel, but I didn't care. He still didn't speak. I knew I had hurt him, but stubbornly refused to look at him. Finally, I could bear his silence no longer. I lifted my gaze without moving my head. His eyes were closed. He was crying silently, tears running along the crease between his cheek and nose, tracing the outline of his top lip before dropping onto the linen of the bed covering. I had never seen him cry and it broke my heart, all the more so that I was the cause of it.

"I'm sorry. I'm so sorry." I whispered it over and over as I held his face in my hands and kissed his brow, his eyes, his tears. He looked at me, his eyes more intensely green than ever.

He spoke in a whisper clouded with emotion. "I have been happier with you, here, than at any other moment in my life." He wiped his face. "I thought, I hoped, you felt the same. You fight to survive, but you're not living, not really. It's as good as being dead already." He rolled onto his back and covered his face with both hands.

I didn't know what to say. As usual, he was right.

We spent the remainder of the day in silence. I busied myself with my herbs and, as it was a beautiful day, I aired the linens on the hill. I even managed to drag the feather mattress out the door and draped it over the woodpile. William made his way up the hill and spent much more time than necessary weeding the garden.

I finally could tolerate it no longer. I folded the linens, placed them on the mattress on the woodpile, and walked slowly toward the garden, toward William.

"William," I began softly, not sure what to say beyond that. He did not look up at me. "William, please look at me." I placed a hand on his head and grabbed a handful of hair in my fingers. It had grown since he had first come to me and curls of dark wrapped around my fingers. I pulled his head back, forcing him to look at me. "If I were ever to be happy, it would be with you. I have never been happy. I don't know how, I think. Maybe it just isn't in my nature."

"Of course it's in your nature. You just haven't learned how."

I released his hair, but kept my fingers on the soft curls.

126

William closed his eyes and moved his head under my fingers, like a cat arching to its master's touch. It struck me that standing there on the hill, with my fingers in his curls, that this was what happiness was. It made me want it more.

"Show me," I whispered.

Later that evening, we lay together. I had my face buried in the curve of his neck, his hands clasping my nape, pulling me tightly against him. We had made love, slowly and tenderly, erasing the hurts of the day. Now, we lay quietly, our breaths coming in time, one with another.

"Are you ready?" William kissed the top of my head.

"Ready for what?"

"Your first lesson. In happiness."

"Oh, not now. I'm much too happy for any lessons now."

"See, you're learning already."

I bit him lightly on the throat. "Very well, lesson number one."

William pulled me closer. "The first lesson—actually, the only lesson—is to trust."

"Trust what? Trust you?"

"Trust me, trust life. Have a wee bit of faith that all will be well. Tell yourself that, no matter what happens, it will all work out. Don't fight it so much. Just let it happen. Trust it."

I turned away from him, laying my head on his arm, my back pressed against his warmth. I absentmindedly played with his fingers, curling and uncurling them one by one.

"Well?"

"Well, I think that it is easy for you to say that. I fight it because I have had to. Maybe you've had time for hope and trust, but I have not. Faith and hope are fine enough for those who don't need it. The rest of us don't depend on it. We know better."

"You don't know so much, Mancy. You say it is easy for me, but what part of my life do you think is easy? I have legs that don't work. I have no money, no hope for income. If it weren't for you, I would end up as a beggar, or worse. I'll never see my family again and my only brother is probably praying I have already died."

"And yet, you're happy?"

"Aye, I am. I'm happy to wake up every morning next to you, to be alive another day. I'm happy watching you work, bundling your plants and tending the garden. And I am happiest lying awake next to you at night, talking about kelpies and dragons and nonsense such as that."

I smiled. "I love that, too. There are so many things I love in this world. Walking in the hills gathering my plants, making salves, working in the garden. And you, I love you—your eyes and the way they crinkle when you smile. And the way you make me laugh. No one has ever made me laugh like you."

"And yet, you are not happy."

I shrugged. "I have moments of happiness, I suppose, but there is always something dark, waiting for me, just over my shoulder or over the hill. It has always been with me, ever since I can remember. I think it is gone sometimes, like when I married William, or when I had Lizzie, and I am so happy that I think I will burst. You know, she was born in the caul, Lizzie was."

I smiled to myself, remembering her birth. Even though I had birthed twice before, I had convinced myself that the boys had entered the world so quickly because they were early. I told myself that this time would be different, that I would have a long, slow labor as many first-time mothers had. I was surprised, then, when I felt myself pushing not long after the first pain. William had barely had time to fetch Isobel and she had just set up her linens when the top of Lizzie's head was visible between my legs. Her head crowned fully with the next push. I reached down to touch her hair, but felt only a slick dampness. I asked Isobel what was wrong with her head, and she laughed as she broke the caul to give her passage into the world. "Nothing, child. She is perfect and will have good luck all her days. Maybe the sight, as well." I held her in my arms, scarcely breathing, afraid that she would break to pieces or, perhaps, disappear if I took my eyes off her. I was distracted, then, by Isobel, who would pause every few moments while cleaning me and changing the linens to flick her wrist, as if trying to shake off a wandering spider or stray hair.

"What is wrong with your wrist?"

Isobel finished tucking a clean cloth under my hips and pulled her sleeve back to look for the offending object. She chuckled as she unwound a section of Lizzie's caul that had managed to wrap itself around her wrist, not once, but twice, like a bracelet.

"She's given me a gift. I've never seen the likes of this before. Oh, Mancy, this is a good sign, a very good sign."

William buried the afterbirth at the threshold of the cottage door, but Isobel asked if she could keep the caul. She dried it and would carry it in her pocket to births for luck. I searched for the little dried scrap in her cottage after they had burned her, but didn't find it. I hoped she had taken it with her, taken it to her death. Not for luck—it was long past time for that—but to have a bit of those who loved her with her at the end.

I told William of her birth and the caul. "I was happy then, at her birth. I didn't believe in the caul, that it would bring her luck. But, I wanted to believe in it. Isobel was so sure. She put that piece of caul in her pocket with every faith in the world that it was magical. I wanted to believe her." I took his hand and placed it at the base of my throat. He traced the outline of my collarbone. I took a deep breath. "But, then there it was again, the darkness, at Lizzie's bedside when she was taking her last breath in my arms, or right behind me, when I was rolling William into his grave. So much for luck. It always comes back for me, no matter what, the darkness."

"*Banish* it, Mancy." His words were spoken forcefully, and for a second, I had a vision of him in battle, standing on his own two legs, strong and tall, fighting for his country, his family, his honor. He must have been impressive in battle.

William continued, "Whatever it is, tell it to go away. Tell it you have no room for it anymore. Replace it with happiness."

"It is not that simple. It is my legacy and you can't deny your legacy."

"That's nonsense. How is it that darkness and fear are your legacy?"

"It is a long story."

"Tell it to me. All of it."

I paused. It was an unspoken story, stored in my memory and heart, wordless and cold. It scared me to give it life, to put a voice to it, to give it power. But, William was right—I was surviving, not living. It was unspeakable, but had to be spoken. And now was the time.

"Tell me, Mancy."

I turned back to face him, but spoke more to his chest than his face. My voice was small, like a child's.

"My name is not Mancy. It is Janet. Named after my mother." Here I paused and looked straight into his eyes. "I am a witch's get."

CHAPTER 26

A nd so, I told him my story, the story of the witch's get. I told him all I remembered, but the memories of a six-year-old lass are changeable and fleeting, impressions more than memories.

My mother was named Janet, and I, her only daughter, was named in her honor. I remember her in patches, her hair, her hands. I remember her voice, and her wordless songs. She called me "bonnie Jane" as we walked through the woods and hills, gathering.

Then I remember the rest. They took her away, from our house, one afternoon. I was clinging to her skirt, fighting with all my might to pull her back to me. The boys were huddled in the corner, the oldest crying and the youngest scared into a silent scream, mouth open with no sound coming out. My father was also there, watching me tear at my mother's clothing. I was strong, even then. He suddenly pulled me back, and I was left clutching a piece of her dress, torn at the hem. And she was gone.

He said nothing about her after that, and struck us if we asked for her. I comforted my brothers the best I knew how, but what could I tell them? I had no words to soothe them, and none for myself.

Then one day, we were taken to her. I don't know where it was. Our father didn't go, only two men who came for us. It was dark and cold and smelled of stale urine and decaying flesh. We watched as she was tortured, her face the one in my dreams, lips clenched, eyes frantic. My brother vomited on the feet of one of the men and was knocked flat by the other. I picked him up and held him tight against me. He buried his face, saliva and vomit dripping from his mouth, against my dress, but they forced him to look at her, as they tried everything they could to break her. When she lost consciousness, they took us back home and dropped us at the door. Our father didn't even acknowledge our return.

The last time I saw her was at her execution. She was placed in a barrel, alive. It was driven through with stakes of metal and then rolled down a hill. At the bottom, it was burned. I don't know what part of this process finally killed her. She made not a sound that I heard, but everything that day was soundless—soundless and slow. We went home with our father—he had been present for the execution—and had dinner, as usual. My brother, the one right below me, spoke my name, asked for the oatcakes at the table. My father turned the table upside down, chairs flying, my brothers wailing. "That name will never be spoken again in this house!" That was his only pronouncement as he left the cottage.

For months, I was nameless. My brothers would occasionally have a slip of the tongue, but it was not long before they learned that it was much less painful just to call me "sister." I had lost both my mother and my name in one fateful day.

Finally, I decided on a new name. We had nothing left of our mother. All evidence of her existence had been removed one night while we slept, before her execution had occurred. And now, even her name was obliterated. But, I knew a secret, one that kept my injured spirit alive. My mother told me once, while we were gathering on the hill, that she, too, had lost her name. She was named Samantha, after her mother, my grandmother. An English name for an English daughter. My grandmother had called her "Mancy" so as to lessen confusion between the two of them. When she had brought Mancy to Scotland, she decided, for the sake of the girl, that she needed a new name, a Scottish name. Thus, Mancy became Janet. My grandmother assumed that Mancy didn't remember the change—she was very young at the time—but, my mother had never forgotten her old name, that other part of her that existed only in a floating memory.

"My name is Mancy," became my mantra, repeated over and over, until all accepted it. My father said nothing of my choice beyond, "That's not a proper name." I knew then that my mother had shared her secret with me and me alone. I rejoiced inwardly every time it was spoken, because it infused our lives with the spirit and memory of my mother, even though I was the only one aware of it.

CHAPTER 27

It was many years later that I learned from Isobel the details of her arrest and execution. We were in the middle of some chore, sorting dried herbs or bundling with twine, perhaps, I don't remember. I do remember that Isobel was furious. The day before, she had been called to heal a sick child, but the woman would not accept her advice, and refused to pay her for her services. Isobel was not one to accept a slight like that quietly. She had thrown a fit at the woman's house, cursing and flinging her arms about. I had tried to calm her on our walk home, but everything I said just made her angrier. It was best to leave it be.

The next day, as we worked, she continued her ranting. I did what I always did, nodded silently, murmuring assent when it was needed. All of a sudden, she stopped midstream and looked at me. "I knew your mother."

I looked at her dumbly. "My mother?"

"You're Janet's girl, are ye not?"

"Aye, I am." I was trying to figure out which line of reasoning led her to this new topic.

She frowned. "It was horrible, what they did to her."

I nodded, still unsure as to where this was leading.

"It surprised me when she was accused. She was always so quiet and minded her own. Everyone liked her."

"Who did it then?"

"Accuse her? You don't know?"

I shook my head.

"Do you remember your neighbors, the ones that lived closest to your cottage?"

I shook my head again, but then a brief recollection came to me. "Did they have little ones, too? A girl my age?"

"Aye, that's them. I'll wager that you two played together."

I did remember snatches of a dark-headed girl with bare feet and a worn, green frock. We used to wander to the stream to look for rocks.

"Anyway, there was a disagreement."

"With my mother?"

"No, with your father. Your neighbors' cow had broken loose and trampled your garden. It was late in the season, no time to replant. Your father was furious. He demanded payment, but these folks were so poor, poorer even than your family."

It was strange to hear her describe my family as poor. I knew we didn't have much, but we always managed with what we had. I thought that we were just like everyone else, in that respect.

"What happened then?"

"Well, ye know your father. He was just as stubborn and spiteful then as he is today. He wouldn't let it go. Your ma tried to smooth it over, make things better, but he wouldn't budge. Things began to happen at the neighbor's house, bad things. Dead animals, a fire in the barn. Then, their child got sick. The lass that was your age. Do ye remember?"

I didn't. I remember wading in the stream with her and nothing beyond that.

"Your mother was called to tend her."

"My mother?"

"Aye."

"Why my mother?"

"She was a healer, didn't ye know that?"

I shook my head again. I knew very little, it seemed.

"She was very good. Had healing in her bones and heart.

135

She had the knack of knowing just what an ailment needed. Sometimes, she wouldn't even have to look at it, she just knew. Anyway, she tried to heal the girl, but she died anyway. That was the last straw for those folks. The husband accused her of witchcraft, of killing their livestock and burning their barn. And of letting the girl die."

"But, she didn't kill their animals or burn their barn, did she?"

"No, of course not. I'd stake my life on someone else in your family having done that. But, there was never proof."

"For her or against her?"

"Neither. And she might have had a defense but for your father."

"*My father?* What did he do?"

Isobel snorted. "It was nothing he did, it was what he chose not to do. He didn't try to stop it, didn't defend her. He just stood and watched."

I remembered the men dragging her out of our house, while our father stood silently by. As a child, I had never thought to question his inaction. It was only in light of Isobel's story that it seemed strange to me.

Isobel continued, "Rumor flew about for years. Many said she must have been a witch, or her husband would have defended her. Others said he was practicing the black magic with her, and that was why he didn't protest when they took her." Isobel cut her gaze toward me to make sure I was listening. "But, the real reason I knew. And it had nothing to do with witchcraft."

She paused, evidently waiting for me to prod her for more information. I wasn't sure I could handle more than I had already been given. I just stared at her. But, nothing would stop her from telling me, even if I hadn't wanted to hear it.

"Your mother was in love with another man and your father knew it. I'm surprised he didn't kill her himself. I never understood how a woman like Janet ended up with your father. So, it was not a surprise to me when she told me about her secret love. I was the only one she confided in. I never told a soul."

"How did my father know then?"

"Well, it wasn't by my tongue, that's for sure. How am I to know? Maybe she wasn't careful, maybe he just figured it out. Men can smell those things out, you know."

"So, when they came for her?"

"Saved him the trouble of doing it himself, I reckon."

I pinched the bridge of my nose with my fingers to prevent the tears that were building there from slipping out.

"All right, lass?"

"Aye," I lied.

Isobel smiled ruefully. "She never confessed though. I'll wager that is why they were so cruel to her. The torture and all, in front of you wee ones. They wanted a confession. But, she never gave it. I heard that she would pray for forgiveness in the middle of the pain, but that when they stopped, she would stick by her story—she was no witch. They never got a confession, but they condemned her anyway. That's why they burned her alive. If she had been contrite, they would have strangled her before they put her in the barrel. She fought them to the end."

A wave of nausea washed over me. I thought of my brother vomiting on the feet of one of my mother's tormentors. "Were you there, Isobel? I don't remember seeing you."

"Oh, lass, how could ye remember anything from that day? Aye, I was there. She was my friend and I owed her that much."

My head was spinning and I remembered how I felt that day, as if I were seeing everything from a distance, blurry and muffled. I wanted to end this discussion, change the subject. But then, a question came to me, one that Isobel would be able to answer. "Isobel, can I ask you something about that day?"

"Of course, lass. Anything."

"Did she make a sound? I didn't hear her make a sound, but I couldn't even hear the barrel rolling down the hill. Did she cry out?"

Isobel smiled, broadly this time. "Not a peep, lass, not a peep."

CHAPTER 28

No more was said of my mother's death for several weeks. Had I dreamed the whole thing? Then Isobel asked me to sort the herbs we had bundled as we spoke that afternoon. As I crushed the dried leaves with a wooden pestle, the smell carried me back to the details of her disclosure, the floating feeling I had experienced and the nausea. It was no dream.

That afternoon, we were called to a birth on the far side of our village. I gathered our supplies and we headed off toward town. Something had been gnawing at me since the day we had spoken of my mother, but I was unable to pin it down. Finally, there on the path, walking side by side with Isobel, our aprons occasionally rustling one against another, I found a voice for my confusion.

"Isobel?"

"Hmm?"

"I was wondering. Why did you tell me about my mother that day? I mean, why didn't you tell me a long time ago? You've known for years. Why did you wait?"

Isobel sighed. "I didn't mean to tell ye at all. I thought it was too much for a lass to bear. After all the talk died down, I thought it was best to forget about the whole thing."

"Then why did you tell me now?"

"Did ye know that there has been talk again? Of witches and such?"

I shook my head. "Where? Here?"

"Aye, here and there. Some folk are stirring things up, talking of the burnings, making trouble. It's the same old story. When times are hard, someone has to be blamed. Might as well be the witches."

"Blamed for what?"

"Whatever is ailing folks at the time. The weather, the crops. This time, it's the fever that's been running through the village that has tongues wagging."

"Aye, but that has naught to do with witches."

"I know that and ye know that. But, it makes folks feel safe to have someone to blame for it."

I was trying to link the strands of reasoning running through this conversation, but, as far as I could make out, she had not answered my question. "I still don't understand. What made you change your mind? About telling me?"

Isobel barked her reply. "Ye dinna ken? Ye are a witch's get. The daughter of a witch. It hasn't been that many years that your mother was burned. People remember, even if they don't speak about it. It will taint you for the rest of your life. There's no escaping that. I tell you to warn you. When the burnings begin again, which they will, they will look to you."

Her words pierced me, just as the iron spikes that had been driven through my mother's bones and flesh. But, unlike my mother's wounds, which led to her horrific demise, my wound would let me live. It would fester inside me, black and heavy, as I accepted my legacy, the legacy of a witch's get, without question. We never spoke of it again.

William listened to my story without interruption. When I had finished, he had only one comment. "They'll have to take me first."

I fell asleep in his arms.

CHAPTER 29

Iknew when I heard the squeaking of the wagon wheels that he had returned. It was daylight, but we were not fully awake. I heard it before William, and jumped up to peek out the door.

"William, sit up," I said, helping him into a seated position on the side of the bed. "It is your brother." My voice was not my own, and sounded as if it were coming from far away, from another's mouth.

William arranged his clothes and I smoothed his hair. It was important to me that he seem healthy and strong. I didn't want his brother to pity him, at least not at first glance. I put my hand on his shoulder and waited.

He pounded on the door and the sound reverberated through me, taking me back to the night he had brought William to me and I had refused to answer. This time, I responded before he had a chance to knock twice.

He regarded me through the open door. "I've come for my brother, if he still lives."

I stood aside from the door to allow him entrance. I immediately had the feeling that I should have never let him in, although I was helpless to prevent it. I walked quickly to William and rested my hand on his shoulder again.

"Our father is asking for you. I have assured him that you

could not have survived, but he has had dreams. He will not rest until he sees you."

"I am touched that you were so optimistic about my chance of survival. I am sorry to disappoint you." William paused. He was smiling, but his eyes were not crinkling. "But, I am not returning. Tell him I am dead."

"Then I will have to take a body as proof. He has seen you alive in his dreams, and will not rest until he sees you, dead or alive."

William stiffened slightly. I could sense he was unsure how to respond. I myself didn't like the talk of returning with a body, as I was quite sure his brother would not be disappointed to do just that.

"Then it seems I don't have a choice."

"No, none. We should leave immediately. It is a long journey. I imagine you don't have much to gather, as I left you with nothing."

"No, I have very little. But, I will be taking my wife."

I squeezed his shoulder tightly, partly to keep myself upright.

The brother looked at me and then back at William, and then laughed. "You've been busy since I left. No matter, I doubt that father will appreciate you bringing home a peasant woman, wife or not. We will not be taking her along."

William hesitated. I knew he was weighing his options, which were much more limited than his brother yet realized. A terror rose in me that was not a stranger. It visited me first when I was forced to watch my own mother burn in the barrel. It came again with Isobel's death and yet again with William's. Each time it had risen and tried to climb out of my throat and shoot out the end of my fingers and toes, exploding into a whirlwind of rage and grief. But, each time it was forced down into my bowels, where it resided, angry and festering, waiting for its release. It had no voice when I was six, watching my mother suffer in agony. It had no voice to speak for Isobel when she was tried and burned when I was a grown woman. But, this time, its voice was present, my throat open and prepared to channel the anger that was demanding to be heard.

As William and his brother faced each other silently, I climbed onto the bed and sat behind William, my arms wrapped around his waist. I buried my face into his back and listened.

"If you will not come willingly, we'll have to take you," the brother was saying, and for the first time, I noticed the presence of another man in the room, the same one who carried William in that first night. He was standing, motionlessly, by the door. I tightened my grip about William's waist and slowly locked my legs around him as well. I was not giving him up without a fight.

I could not discern William's emotion in his voice, and I could not see his face. I have since had to fill in his expression in my mind, as I did the moment he first faced his useless legs. Sometimes I think he must have been resigned to leaving—there really was nothing either one of us could do about it. Other times, I imagine his face reflecting fear or anger, or perhaps, desperation. Whatever he was feeling, his voice was calm and steady, which caused my panic to rise even more.

His next words ripped me apart. "You'll have to take me either way for I cannot go on my own, even if I chose to." His brother cocked his head to one side, and then his eyes widened. He nodded to the man at the door, who came toward the bed.

I was ready. I used all my strength in my arms and legs to pull William toward me. His brother grabbed me from behind, his arm around my neck, his hand clasping my wrist. I tucked my chin quickly enough to enable me to bite him hard on the forearm. He cursed me, pulling his arm back quickly, my wrist still in his grasp, just at the moment the other man had managed to unlock my legs from around William's lap. I fell backward, off the bed and hit my head hard on the floor. I heard the thud and then could hear or see nothing for a second. When I could focus again, I saw the brother's heavy boots next to me. I could not see William's legs dangling, but could hear him calling my name. Now he sounded panicked.

"Let's go." It was the brother's voice. He turned to step around the bed, toward the door, but I grabbed his ankle as he stepped. It was his turn to fall, hard, and on his face. I was on him in a second.

"I will kill you," I heard a voice say before realizing that it was my own.

He managed to turn onto his back before I straddled him, but he did not have time to protect himself. I used my very large hands to encircle his throat. Once again, I found my strength useful as I dedicated every muscle I had to choking him.

I was muttering as I squeezed. "You'll not take him from me." I said this again and again, and watched as his face grew dusky, the same color that I had seen on babies whose heads were out, but whose shoulders were stuck. It was an ominous color, one I had always dreaded seeing. Now, I was intentionally bringing it about. There is no excuse for what I did. I had become a wild animal, a mad being whose capacity for rational thought was obliterated by rage. I could feel my own blood pounding in my temples and my eyeballs bulge, as he struggled. Would I have killed him? Without a doubt, but for being jerked back by an arm around my own throat. The other man pulled me off of him and flung me back, this time against the bed.

William's brother slowly sat up, coughing and gagging. He glared at me. His eyes were as I remembered, as green as his brother's. But cold, and full of hate. "You are a witch, a demon." He hurled the words at me and I caught them in mid-air and hurled them back.

"If I be a witch, then I curse you to damnation. Your soul will rot in hell."

I could taste blood in my mouth, from what I didn't know, and felt a sob coming up as I spat these words out. He was walking out the door by the time I could get myself off the floor. I started after him, but went back into the cottage, grabbed the jar of comfrey salve from the table, and ran to the cart as it was pulling away.

William was in the back, hunched over, still calling me. "Mancy," he said with the softness I knew so well.

"They won't know how to take care of you." My words were choked. "They have to turn you, move your legs."

"I'll be fine. I know what to do." He was trying to calm me, and himself as well.

I was walking behind the cart now, holding his hand in mine. "You need your salve, for the bedsores." I handed him the jar as I trotted to keep up.

"I'll come back for you, Mancy. Don't leave. Wait for me." William's hand slipped from mine.

I was losing ground with the quickening pace of the cart. "I'll wait. I promise." But, then, I ran once more as fast as I could run and reached him again. "Give me your name," I said. "What is your name?"

He smiled at me, eyes crinkling. "William, don't you know. You named me. I am your husband, William."

Of course, I knew. I had always known.

CHAPTER 30

I stood in the path until the cart was no longer in sight, and then stumbled back toward the cottage. I remember stopping at the garden to pull a weed that had strayed into my cabbage. I left the door open and lay on the bed, sinking into the feather mattress, our mattress, still warm from where we had been sleeping, wrapped in each other's arms. I nuzzled my face into the linen sheets, inhaling his scent, which so permeated everything he had touched. Waves of nausea washed over me, come out of nowhere, and I retched off the side of the bed, not even attempting to aim for the jar on the stool. I fell back into the mattress and let myself slide into darkness.

I don't know how much time passed before Annie found me. I awoke to her full, open face staring at me in the dusky light. Her ever-present smile was not there, and her bottom lip trembled slightly as she looked at me, stroking my hair off my face.

"They took him," I said.

"I know. I saw them leave down the path."

"He wasn't William. He wasn't my husband. I lied to you about everything."

She shrugged and smiled feebly. "I knew that. I'm not totally daft."

Tears began to stream, even as I struggled to contain them. "I'm so sorry. I've been awful to you."

"Hush. Enough. We've plenty to deal with without all that nonsense." She wet a cloth and wiped my face and forehead. She tried to smile again, with little success. Something wasn't being said, something she was trying to hide behind the forced smiles. "What is it, Annie?"

Her lip trembled again and she looked at me. "When I saw them taking him, I realized that something was dreadfully wrong. I called to him, called his name, but he wouldn't look up, wouldn't look at me. I don't think he even heard me. I followed them down the path into the village. Oh, Mancy, it is not good. The cart stopped at the inn. But, then he went to the Kirk. He has made a charge against you."

"Who? William?" I was confused, still nauseated and my head had begun to pound.

"No, the other man. In the boots. He marched into the Kirk and accused you of being a witch."

Having spent so many years dreading this moment, I was amazed that these words impacted me so little. I sank back into the bed and closed my eyes. My legacy had come to collect its due. But, it didn't matter now anyway. Annie sat with me until they came to take me.

I was still in William's old clothes when they came for me. I had always supposed I would go dressed properly, wearing my dress and stays and with my head covered, but they arrived much more quickly than I had anticipated and would not even allow me to collect anything to take with me. I did manage to grab my plaid on the way out the door.

Annie was inconsolable, tears streaming down her face, but she managed to utter, "I'll be round to check on you, tomorrow first thing."

I gave her a weak smile as they ushered me roughly out the door.

As it turned out, it didn't matter that I hadn't dressed properly, as they took my clothes from me in the steeple. I was allowed to keep my plaid, and was given a threadbare smock. I was the only human occupant of the steeple at the time, although from the looks of the droppings on the floor, more than one warm-blooded critter shared space with me. The bed was a mattress of straw, covered with a thin sheet. My captors, the two men who had come on behalf of the Kirk to arrest me at my house, watched as I disrobed, grinning. The heavier of the two was actually salivating—he kept swallowing hard. The other man was slighter and twitchy. He wanted to stare and salivate as well, but was unable to hold his gaze on me for more than a few seconds. He finally looked at my plaid, which was lying on the straw.

I ignored their stares, wrapped my plaid around me, and took refuge on the mattress in the corner. I needed to vomit again, but refused to do so in front of the jailers. I breathed slowly through my nose, and concentrated on keeping the contents of my stomach where they belonged. The men hung around a bit more, but must have been disappointed in my lack of reaction, and left. I pulled my plaid tight and lay down to sleep.

CHAPTER 31

I was awakened the next morning by Annie's voice. Somehow she had finagled her way into the steeple. She spoke without drawing a breath, as if she were trying to cram an infinite number of pronouncements in a decidedly finite span of time.

"Here's some porridge and a few eggs," she said, drawing them out of her plaid. "You're freezing cold. Wrap up tighter. I have been so worried about you. I can't stay long and they might not let me see you again after today. Don't despair, Mancy. No matter what happens." She finally paused. "All will be well." She said these words slowly, but without conviction. She hesitated again. "I've been doing some asking around. He said you admitted to being a witch."

"Who said?"

"The man in the boots."

"William's brother."

"That devil is his brother?"

"Aye, I'm afraid he is. Without the brotherly affection. I don't think he cares for me very much, either," I added, trying to make Annie smile.

She did not. "He has accused you of cursing William, of making him lame."

"What?" My ire began to rise and, for a moment, I could

feel his throat under my fingers and see his mottled face, eyes bulging with fear.

"He says you have entered into a pact with the Devil."

I closed my eyes. The only devil I had ever had occasion to have dealings with was my very accuser and our pact was William, to tend him and keep him among the living. I smiled to myself. That I had done well.

"Annie, there's something I must tell you." I paused. "I'm with child." I laughed at the shocked look on Annie's face.

"By William?"

I laughed again. "Of course, by William. Who else?"

I waited as Annie processed this possibility. She recovered quickly. "Does he know?"

"No, I was going to tell him that morning, the morning they took him." My laughter was gone now, sucked out of my throat by the thought. "I wasn't sure until that day. My moon was late, but I wasn't sure until I started vomiting every morning. That's a good sign, right?"

Annie laughed and hugged me. "Of course, you know that! Oh, my child, I have to get you out of this place."

I shook my head. "It's not possible. I know what's to come. There's no escape now."

"You don't know that, Mancy. Give me time."

Time. How much or how little I had was the one thing I wasn't sure of.

I kept Annie in view from the small window in the steeple as she strode through the churchyard, skirts bustling with each determined step, her head covering slightly askew. I had to smile. At that moment, I had fallen in love with her, much as I had fallen in love with Maggie as I cradled her in my arms. More importantly, I knew Annie loved me. It was evident in the purposefulness of her march through the courtyard. If anyone could help me, it would be Annie. I held her figure in my gaze until she turned the corner into the street.

Then I noticed the cemetery. Directly beyond the courtyard, through which Annie had just passed, lay the Kirk's cemetery, the same one in which Maggie was buried. I thought about Maggie, cold and still in her grave, and about my mother and Isobel, who were given no grave at all, their ashes shoveled out unceremoniously and disposed of who knows where. I thought of my boys and little Lizzie, buried in my village and William, lying under the woodpile with his flute.

At that moment, my fear was gone. I saw them all, knew they were there waiting for me. How could I fear the journey? They had all been brave enough to venture there, to pave the way for me. And William's God was there as well, residing in the heavens. For the first time in my life, I decided to speak to Him. Not a prayer, exactly, just a request.

"Keep him safe. If You are there, keep him safe."

CHAPTER 32

The next few days blurred together, indistinguishable one from another. For the first day or so, I was left alone. I was given pottage, stale and cold, and water. I spent most of the daylight hours trying to remember, to commit to memory every detail of my time with William, from the first creak of the wagon wheels in front of my cottage to watching him disappear from view on the path. I thought about our day on the hill, by the garden, when I first kissed him, loved him. I remembered wanting to put that day, the blue skies, the green of the hills, in a jar to be taken off the shelf for just such times as these.

The nights were spent trying to stay warm, shivering under my plaid and the poor excuse for a blanket they had given me. Then the other memories would come, and I would find myself a wee girl, watching my mother writhe in agony as they crushed her legs in the boots, her teeth clenched together, struggling vainly not to scream out, so as not to scare me. Try as I might, I could not take the jar off the shelf at night. It was too high and the lid was on too tight.

Instead, I would scrunch my eyes closed and focus on the wee one floating in my belly. I was amazed how deeply rooted this one was. The others seem to lose their hold so easily. With them, I would lie in the bed, motionless and scarcely breathing, trying not to jostle them. William would tiptoe around the cottage, doing all of the chores, cooking the meals. At night, he would sleep on the floor next to the bed. It made not a whit of difference, of course, and before long, I would see the smear of blood and feel the pains in my womb that meant I would be denied motherhood, yet another time.

This tiny kernel was a tough one. He had held on tight while I slugged it out with William's brother. He dug in even deeper as I was thrown in the steeple and made not one peep about the cold and hunger. I fell in love with his strength, his tenacity. I spent hours composing him in my mind, his features melding and flowing, belonging sometimes to William and other times to me, but mostly they were William. I conjured him up as a baby or a lad of ten or an old man, always with green eyes still sparkling. Then, the bitter cold of the steeple would bring me back to the harsh reality that his destiny was inextricably interwoven with my own. These were the only times I wept.

I don't know how many days I was there before it began. I was already weak from the cold and hunger and nauseated from the pregnancy. As night fell, my captors came into the steeple. There were the two jailers who had been taking pleasure in my suffering up to that point. This time, another man was with them. He was above them, somehow, dressed in finer clothes. He had an air of certainty about him, almost an arrogance. The other two men obviously answered to him.

I regarded them from the little nest I had dug out for myself in the straw.

The heavyset man spoke. "Up, witch."

I considered resisting him, but decided against it. I stood.

"I hope you've had plenty of rest 'cause that'll be the last for awhile."

I had expected this, of course. One of the most insidious instruments of torture utilized in Scotland was not forged of metal. Indeed, it had no form at all. I had heard of it. It had been used on Isobel and, most likely, on my own mother as well. I was to be watched and walked, not allowed to sleep. For those of you who doubt its effectiveness, I assure you it is as horrifying as the most hideous instrument crafted from iron.

"Walk, witch."

Those words began the ordeal. I was not permitted to sleep, or even sit, possibly because if I had sat for more than two seconds together I would have nodded off immediately. I was given sparse amounts of food and a few sips of water. The two jailers took turns watching me in shifts, jabbing me with their sticks when I faltered, nodding off on my feet. The third man in the fine clothes came in from time to time to watch. I finally realized why he was there—he would be doing the pricking, searching my body for the Devil's mark with his pins. The Devil's mark was insensate, with no blood issuing forth, even with the pin driven all the way in. It would be proof of an alliance with the Devil, should it be found.

I would like nothing better than to lie to you now and tell you that I remember nothing of what followed. But, the truth is that I remember all of it, every detail. It is imprinted in my memory as indelibly as the night William and I made the salves, or the afternoon on the hill when I first loved him. But, just as the details of those days were crisp and clear, the memories from my time in the steeple are blurred and cloudy, floating in and out of my conscious mind. Were they real, those moments that linger in my soul, or the remnants of the hallucinations that set in within a few days of being watched? I don't suppose it matters, really.

I knew what all the walking would lead to and I knew what they wanted from me—a confession. I had never understood why so many women had supposedly confessed, but it was becoming clear to me quickly. I had figured I would be able to withstand sleep deprivation better than most—I was a midwife, after all, used to endless hours guiding women through their births. I had many times been called from one birth directly to the next, with time only to restock my herb chest and change into a clean dress. When Lizzie was still alive, I would then have to come home to my mothering duties, which were never ending, no matter how little sleep I had had the night before. Still, the desire to sleep this time, exacerbated by the cold and hunger hit me soon, and hard. I would have given anything to lie down, even on that paltry amount of straw that was my bed, and close my eyes. My lack of guilt began to seem insignificant compared to the overwhelming desire to sleep, to dream. The last conscious thoughts I remember were an inner struggle, part of me arguing for sleep and the rest of me resisting. It was a moot argument, for the hallucinations were to win out in the end.

The odd thing about hallucinations is that they seem so real at the time. Looking back, I can assure you that the men in charge of my captivity had no horns on top of their heads nor fangs growing from their mouths. But there they were, horrifying and fascinating, and as they taunted me and prodded me, I couldn't help but stare at them, wondering how they were able to close their mouths with their protruding teeth and marveling at the shiny brilliance of their horns. I even reached out to touch one of them, causing them to erupt in callous laughter at my curiosity. As time went on, my little jail changed into a mighty forest, dark and ominous, deep black on all sides.

My two captors, devils now, resplendent in black with cloven hooves to accompany their horns, had multiplied into a company of hundreds, dancing in circles about me, poking me, laughing at me. When I tried to defend myself, blindly swinging at the swirl of black, they laughed all the more, cackling with glee at my obvious distress. I finally gave up, closed my eyes, and stood still in the middle of the dancing demons.

All of a sudden there was silence. The whirlwind subsided as quickly as it had started. The legions of demons turned in unison to face an approaching figure. He was, I knew, the Devil himself. I had told William I had never seen him and I probably wouldn't know him if I ever saw him, but that was not true. I knew him immediately, felt his presence in my bones and his chill in my blood. Even though I kept my eyes closed tight, I could see him in my mind's eye, and I knew why he was there. He wanted me. He wanted me for his very own. He wanted to claim me like a prize, and I had no control over the taking. It was to be, whether

I wanted it or not. I then knew how all of those other women confessed so readily. He had come for them also.

The demons in black parted silently to allow his passage. He approached me without words, his hand gently stroking my cheek. I turned from him, my eyes still squeezed tightly closed. The demons cackled anew, but he silenced them with a look.

"Look at me, witch."

I had no choice but to obey. His voice was alluring, smooth, and resonant. I turned to face him.

"Open your eyes."

I did as he told me. He was there, practically touching my face. His breath was not ice cold, as I had expected, but warm on my cheek. He was magnificent to my eyes, handsome and horrifying all at once. I could do nothing but stare.

His hands, warm like his breath on my cold, raw skin, began their exploration. At first he traced the outline of my body through the threadbare shift, but then the shift disappeared, as quickly as if a cold wind blew it off my body. His hands were now exploring my body without restraint. His touch should have repulsed me, but the warmth compelled me instead, and I moved under his fingers, against my own will. Peals of laughter rang in my ears.

In a moment, I was no longer standing, but was on all fours, his hands no longer warm, but burning hot, like embers on my skin.

"Who do you serve, witch?"

I wanted to tell him, to scream, "No one. I serve no one." But, the words would not come. The burning intensified, and sharp pains radiated down my spine, between my shoulder blades. I wanted to cry out, but nothing would come out. My mouth was open, with the same silent scream I remember on my little brother's face the day they took my mother. The heat permeated my body, down my spine, through my belly and into my groin. I knew then that I told William yet another lie about the Devil, because his member was as searing as his hands, burning me through and through. I heard sobs coming from afar, and realized they were my own.

"I serve Him. I confess."

The forest disappeared. I was lying naked on the floor of the steeple.

My tormentors were gone. I fumbled on the floor for what remained of the shift and wrapped myself in it. I crawled to the pile of straw and fell asleep.

CHAPTER 33

The next morning, the jailer woke me with a jab of his stick. "Up, you. Time to go."

I didn't argue. There was no sense in it. I was numb from cold and hunger, aching from lack of sleep. At this point, death would be a respite from this nightmare. My only regret was that my death would snuff out the life growing inside me. This little one was amazingly strong to have survived all I had been through, but there was no help for it now. We would both perish and William would never know that he had fathered this tough little kernel. I closed my eyes to the thought and followed the jailer into the daylight.

After days in the darkness of the steeple, my eyes could not manage the sunlight, even though the day was overcast. I shielded them with one hand, and stumbled slightly, my bare feet raw and numb, not bearing my weight. I braced for a jab from the jailer, but, instead, a hand took my own and steadied me. I had not expected any kindness from those who were soon to delight, however morbidly, in my death and I felt tears swelling from the surprise. The hand held fast, and through a squint, I could make out a worn, strong hand, clasping mine tight. Another hand I could feel at my waist, practically supporting me, as I struggled to keep my balance, my mind blearily trying to make sense of the moment. Unable to do so, I stopped stock-still.

"Slowly, child, slowly. But, do keep moving. At this rate, we will never reach the cart."

I lifted my gaze from the hand and found myself staring into William's face, aged and lined, framed with white hair. The same green eyes crinkled as he smiled.

"Onward then? Oh, dear. Andrew, catch her."

For at that point, my head began to swim and darkness was creeping into my line of vision. A large man, who evidently was a few paces behind me, swept me up in his arms and carried me to a waiting cart. It was the same cart that had brought William to my cottage that fateful night and the same one that bore him away only a few days earlier. The man, Andrew, placed me gently in the back of the cart and climbed on in front. The white-haired man climbed into the back and sat next to me.

"I don't understand," was all I could think to say.

"There's naught to understand. The charges against you have been dropped. The fool who brought them has admitted they were false accusations." A sadness crept into his smile. "He has been dealt with."

"What happens to me now?"

He smiled again and leaned closer toward me, his answer given slowly and softly.

"Well, my son says you tended him very dearly. 'Tis our turn to do the same for you. You are one of us now."

Less than a few hours later, I found myself lying in the back of the cart on the feather mattress—our mattress—as we wended our way to William, to home. We had stopped by the cottage long enough to gather my few possessions. William's father had apologized for not bringing a proper carriage to collect me, but had brought the cart instead so as to have room for my things. He was surprised when I asked for only a few precious items— my herb chest, the little wooden mallet tucked inside, and a few articles of clothing in a linen bag, including the breeches and tunic I had first dressed William in when he came to me.

"Is there nothing else you wish to keep?"

I shook my head, but then thought of the mattress. "If there is room…" He sent Andrew with me back into the cottage to bundle up the mattress. He folded it in half, as much as it would be folded, and as he lifted it onto his shoulders, a wave of recognition came over me. I knew the arm that was steadying the mattress, for it was the one that had yanked me off of William's brother, breaking my grip around his throat. Andrew had been in this cottage twice before, once to deposit William onto my bed and once to collect him again.

He must have sensed my recognition, because he stopped, mattress balanced on his shoulders, eyes cast downward. "I hope I didna hurt you when I threw you back like that."

"I wasn't hurt. Not really."

He gave a half-smile. "You woulda killed him?"

"Without a doubt."

He smiled again and lumbered to the cart. I glanced quickly around the cottage to see if there was anything I had forgotten. In that instant, I saw it all before me—Maggie lying on the bed, spitting orders at me, William on the same bed, stinking and filthy. And then a jumble of images—dandelions, egg yolks splattered on a tunic, the wooden hammer, pounding, pounding. I smelled lavender and William's scent, mixed with my ripeness and oil. I smelled birth as well, and knew that it was the smell that was to be in a few short months, when our baby would be born onto our feather mattress. It would be the smell of blood and fluids, sensual and deep, fresh as the grass and ancient as the earth itself. As I turned to leave, I remembered one last item worth taking with me. I went to the hearth and retrieved the leather pouch from behind the stone.

Annie practically ran over me as I made my way to the cart. Her grin was back where it belonged, and she grabbed me around the neck, almost strangling me in the process. "Mancy! You're going!" She squeezed me tighter, laughing and crying at the same time.

"Aye, I suppose I am. It has all happened so quickly."

"I was so worried. But, now all is well. You're going to be with William again."

It was the first time since leaving the steeple that I had allowed myself to consider this, that within the next few days— or would it be hours?—I would be in his arms again, inhaling his scent. I felt tears stinging again.

Annie hadn't drawn a breath. "I'll miss you, more than you will know. But, Mancy, I am so happy for you. Come to see me—I want to see your wee one." She stopped short, and for a moment her smile faded. "I'll miss you so."

"I'll miss you, too." I again felt an overwhelming love for Annie. I would miss her exuberance for all of life, mine as much as her own. "You've been a good friend. My only friend."

"Hush. Enough of that. Go, would you." She hugged me one last time and shoved me toward the cart. "Go."

The rhythm of the cart lulled me into a trancelike state. William's father had forced some food and water into me and sat next to me, humming an indistinct melody. I almost slipped into sleep when the question leapt into my mind. I cleared my throat, unsure how to address him.

"Yes, lass."

"Might I ask you a question?"

"Of course, child."

"What is your son's name?"

He paused. "Robert."

"Robert," I repeated to myself. I closed my eyes and called William's face to my mind, trying to match it to this newly discovered name. Robert. It had such a different sound, harsher somehow—not the lilting softness of William. I sighed, wondering if I would ever be able to reconcile this dissonance. William's father responded to the sigh.

"Don't worry, lass. He'll not bother you again. He's on a boat to the Americas. A bit of hard work will set him straight enough." He shook his head. "I don't know what happened to that one. He was a good lad, but no more."

"Oh, no. Not that son. The other one." William's father looked at me quizzically. "The one I tended. What is his name?"

"William."

"Aye, William. What is his name?"

William's father smiled bemusedly and tried again. "His name is William."

"But, that was the name I gave him…."

"Well, that might be, but his mother and I gave it to him first, on the day of his birth. After his father." His eyes crinkled as he spoke.

So, he had told me the truth. His name was William and he was my husband.

EPILOGUE

I told you I wasn't beginning at the beginning and I'll not end at the end. For my story went on for many years, the story of my life with William and our children, of happiness and laughter, and in my life, finally, peace. But, I only promised you the voice of the witch. And the end of that story began with that cart ride home. It wasn't done with immediately, of course. For years, I carried the weight of my legacy. How had I managed to cheat my fate and survive, when so many others—Isobel, my own dear mother—had faced horrific ends? So even though I was happy, so very happy, with William and our children, I always felt the burden of that happiness, of having survived.

That burden was at long last lifted by the words of our little kernel, who surprised her mother by being a ginger-headed lass. Turns out, the Jew who was not a gypsy knew more than I gave him credit for. We named her Jane, after her grandmother, and she was, at that moment, sorting the flowers we had picked that morning, tying them into little bundles. I was helping her and William was sitting quietly at the little table we had set up outside, watching us. Our son, William, was scampering about, throwing rocks, chasing the dogs. We had named him William, even though his father had objected that it would be confusing to have so many Williams under one roof. We had gone through every possible configuration of name under the Scottish sun, but I always came back to William. After all, all of the truly wonderful men in my life had answered to that name. I didn't want to take chances with any other.

It was a glorious day, chilly, but clear with ice-blue skies. Jane was humming as she worked, and I smiled as I caught a piece of melody that my mother sang to me. I wished they could meet—my mother and her namesake—that we could have an afternoon in the hills, gathering plants and chatting.

Jane paused in her bundling and looked up at me with a question in her green eyes. She opened her mouth and then closed it again without speaking, her hands still quiet. I waited.

"Maw?"

"Yes, my heart?"

"Did ye know that plants can talk?"

I glanced at William. He was smiling.

"Of course, my love. I have always known that."

At that very moment, with the innocent inquiry of a child, I knew there was no guilt to be borne in my survival. I had not cheated my legacy, the one that others had imposed on me. For I wasn't a witch's get, after all. I was a healer's get. My legacy wasn't one of fire and metal, but one of plants and all things green and growing, of bluebottles and heather in the Scottish hills. It was a legacy of babies slipping into my hands and broken collarbones knitting under my care. It was a legacy I had inherited, along with my brown hair and hazel eyes, from my mother and her mother before her. And now it would be the legacy of my daughter. It would be hers to give to her daughters yet unborn, waiting still and silent, until they too can make their journey to this realm and learn the ways.

So, here I am. I am sure you are wondering what it is like here. I will tell you—it looks just like Scotland. There are the hills and the heather and the wind slapping my cheeks pink. I have been very busy since I arrived. It turns out that there is quite a bit of work here for healers. There are many of us—healers—from every part of the world and we still can't keep up with the work.

Annie is here to help me. Not help, actually, for just as in life, she watches as I work, chatting endlessly, trying to make me smile. She was never a healer, but she saved me, nonetheless. For I found out from William that it was she who told him of my arrest. She had followed his brother into the Kirk. Her outgoing nature, which had made me cringe so many times, had resulted in a vast web of connections in the village, and it didn't take much for her to learn the details of the charges against me. Luckily, Robert and his man had stopped by the inn for ale, giving her opportunity to warn William. He said the ride home was unbearable, heavy with the knowledge that my life hung in the balance, each bump and rut in the road that slowed their progress tightening the knot around his heart. He could give his brother no clue that he was aware of my fate, for he was sure that Robert would just as soon leave him on the side of the road as not. His only hope, my only hope, was for him to reach his father. His father had rescued me, but it was truly Annie who had saved me.

So, here we are together, Annie chatting and me healing. I began my healing with the witches. I met them one by one and called them each by name—Margaret, Anna, Katherine, Chiara. How many were there? It seemed to be as many as the stars. It mattered not, for I tended them one by one.

For Anna, whose breasts were cut from her body and shoved into her mouth before they burned her, I chose calendula, soothing calendula, and comfrey, the healer of wounds. For Margaret, whose daughter was tortured in front of her to induce her confession, I chose dandelion and nettles, to nourish her tormented spirit. For my own mother, I used beautiful marigold, to cleanse her very soul. I tended them one by one, and held their hands in mine and kissed their faces. Then, I bathed us in lavender, for peace, and plaited flowers in our hair, for joy. And we were whole again.

But, my work is not finished—far from it. They still arrive, brides burned alive for lack of dowry and baby girls who have pebbles stuffed into their mouths at birth. Torture victims from countries led by despotic madmen and children tortured in their own homes by their own parents. Of course, there are many who don't need me, who are greeted with loving arms by those who have been waiting for them. They are the lucky ones whose lives did not leave them broken and in despair.

For the others, we are still here, infusing our oils and making our salves. We have all of the plants of the earth at our disposal, all of the remedies of humankind, but it is our love that we pour into our potions and brew into our teas. That is the best healer of all.

I can almost hear William saying, "But, who heals you, Mancy? Who touches you?" And I answer, "I am already healed—healed by the love of a man with no legs, who taught me how to laugh and live and breathe again." There will be you who will want to know if I have found him, if he is here with me. The honest truth—for lies do not serve me here—is that I haven't had time to look for him. If you all could somehow find a way to end the cruelty and torture, then eventually my work would be done. As it is, there is no end in sight. God, the very One I was accused of being enemy to, is as I imagined. He is not the God of fire and metal, but the God of healing and plants, and all things growing and beautiful. He is the One who gave me my healing and I cannot deny it ever again. I owe Him that much. After all, He answered my prayer, which was more of a request really. He kept him safe.

Made in the USA
Charleston, SC
08 August 2014